The Castle Corona

SHARON CREECH

BLOOMSBURY

LONDON NEW DELHI NEW YORK SYDNEY

Bloomsbury Publishing, London, New Delhi, New York and Sydney

First published in Great Britain in 2007 by Bloomsbury Publishing Plc
50 Bedford Square, London WC1B 3DP

www.bloomsbury.com

Bloomsbury is a trademark of Bloomsbury Publishing Plc

First publishing in the United States of America in 2007
by Joanna Cotler Books
an imprint of HarperCollins Publishers

This paperback edition published in June 2014

A CIP catalogue record for this book is available from the British Library

ISBN 978 1 4088 4803 6

1 3 5 7 9 10 8 6 4 2

Printed in Great Britain by CPI Group (UK) Ltd, Croydon CR0 4YY

'A delightful book. The narrative progresses like a picturesque and finely drawn puzzle that is satisfyingly pieced together'
Guardian

'Wholly enchanting with wishes and dreams pursued'
School Librarian

'A novel where simplicity of style and complexity of message are cleverly matched'
Irish Times

'An insightful social commentary wrapped up in an appealing and engaging fairy-tale package'
Carousel

'An entertaining adventure'
Sunday Herald

'Transcends both time and culture'
School Librarian

'Wonderful fairy tale . . . A delightful story filled with secrets and dreams'
Family Interest

'*The Castle Corona* is a story of royal proportions, offering readers a unique take on a classic fairy tale; loveable, fascinating characters; and an intriguing, spirited plot line'
BookPage

Books by Sharon Creech

(In alphabetical order)

A Fine, Fine School
Absolutely Normal Chaos
Bloomability
Chasing Redbird
Fishing in the Air
Granny Torrelli Makes Soup
Hate That Cat
Heartbeat
Love That Dog
Pleasing the Ghost
Replay
Ruby Holler
The Boy on the Porch
The Castle Corona
The Great Unexpected
The Unfinished Angel
The Wanderer
Walk Two Moons
Who's That Baby?

For

Pearl and Nico

Annie, Sandra Kay, and Mary

Alex, Andrew and Madeleine

Witt and Jula

Johnathan, Kaitlyn, Meghan, Lauren and Morgan

Contents

In a Towering Castle . . .

A Story Was Told . . .

Once there was a **Castle,** high on a hill,
and a **King** who longed for a nap
and a **Queen** who yearned for solitude
and a **Prince** who loved poetry
and a **Princess** who loved herself
and a **Spare Prince** who loved his sword
and a **Hermit** who was wise.

And there was a **Village**, down in the valley,
and a **Peasant Girl** who dreamed of flying
and a **Peasant Boy** who dreamed of horses
and a **Master** who dreamed of turnips
and an **Old Woman** who kept secrets.

Long Ago
and Far Away . . .

꩜ 1 ꩜

A Discovery

A young peasant girl and her brother kneeled in the smooth gray stones on the edge of the river, filling wooden buckets with water for their master.

"What if we built a raft," the girl asked, "and sailed down the river?"

"Ho!" the boy said. "What would we find?"

"That the river winds round and round—"

"And up and down—"

"—until it reaches the Castle Corona, it does!"

This was a familiar game for the pair, and they would have gone on longer, speculating about the white horses and the golden goblets and the jewels that they would find in the castle, but they were interrupted by a fierce pounding of the earth: horses coming fast along the path behind them.

Through the trees they saw a black horse, ridden by a black-cloaked rider. The rider's whip slapped with hard *thwacks* against the horse's side. A few minutes later, more horses followed, ridden by the King's Men, their golden medallions shimmering on their red cloaks. "Halt! Thief!" one rider shouted. "Halt, in the name of the King!"

"*Ooh!*" whispered the boy. "A thief?"

"A *thief*?"

"And if they catch him—"

"They will slice off his head—"

"—and chop him to bits!"

The pair snatched their buckets and hurried up the bank, crossing the path which the riders had taken. They had just entered the woods beyond when the girl said, "Look—in the leaves."

There, amid last autumn's brown leaves, was a leather pouch with the King's seal on it.

“Dare we?” whispered the boy.

“Here, back in here,” the girl said, snatching the pouch and leading her brother into a thicket, where they paused and listened. All was quiet.

2

If Only . . .

High above the banks of the wide and winding Winono River stood the spectacular Castle Corona. In daylight the castle's stone walls reflected glints of gold, and in the moonlight they sparkled with slivers of silver, so that for miles around, by day or night, the splendid castle glittered. Castle Corona was home to King Guido and Queen Gabriella and their three children, and because it takes many people to attend to and protect a king and his family, the castle was also home to hundreds of servants and soldiers, gardeners and groomsmen, and to their families.

If you were a poor peasant in one of the

outlying villages—if you were, say, in the straw sandals of young Pia or her brother, Enzio, who were filling buckets at the river—you might catch sight of the castle and envy its inhabitants. You might think, as Pia and Enzio did, *If only I could be a princess or a prince . . . If only I could wear clothes spun with gold . . . If only I could ride white ponies with golden bangles . . . If only, if only—then my life would be perfect and beautiful and easy. . . . If only, if only . . .*

The master of Pia and Enzio, who had a stomach like a barrel and a ragged scar which ran down his face like a twisted snake, once told Pia and Enzio, "Life is not a fairy tale, you dirty beetles. These wishes, these "if onlys," won't do you much good, and they might do you some harm, especially if your master is impatient with such daft dreams and will whack you on the back of your knees with a leather strap if he catches you daydreaming instead of tending to your chores."

What neither the master nor the young peasants Pia and Enzio knew was that the glittering King and his family did not have such perfect or beautiful or easy lives, even though it might seem that way to outsiders. They sometimes thought, *If only I could be a poor, anonymous peasant . . . If only I didn't have to wear these heavy golden clothes . . . If only I didn't have to always smile and be polite and make decisions . . . If only I could choose my own friends and do what I liked . . . If only, if only . . .*

Like the peasants whose wishes do not do them any good, so the wishes of kings and queens and princes and princesses often do not do them any good, for they are born to be what they are, and there is no escaping it.

Not usually.

3

The Meek, The Spare, The Spoiled

Above the Castle Corona one summer day, a string of clouds, like the wings of downy white doves, whisked across a pale blue sky, gently but purposefully sailing toward some distant oasis. Prince Gianni was kneeling on a red velvet cushion, his elbows resting on the cool stone sill, his chin in his hands. "Another day, another sky," he said to the air.

Prince Gianni, fourteen years of age, was a tall, gangly beanpole of a boy, with black, untamed locks and deep-set ebony eyes. There was a dreamy look about his face, a certain softness around the eyes and the mouth that was not particularly princely, but he had the King's chiseled jaw, and from the time he could stand, he had been trained to carry himself in a rigid, upright stance.

"You must walk like royalty," his Tutor of Walking had told him. "Stand like tree, see? But without branches jutting out. Branches down by trunk, see? And when you walk—"

"Trees don't walk," the Prince had said.

"Your Royal Highness, Heir to the Throne of Corona, is correct, it is true. Trees do not walk. You stand like tree. You *walk* like prince. I show you." And the Tutor of Walking had demonstrated a princely stride.

Now, from the courtyard below drifted the heady fragrance of roses and honeysuckle. Two yellow birds circled a rosemary bush, diving in and out, chittering as they swooped playfully. A servant girl darted from one dark doorway to another, her arms full of dirty laundry.

Prince Gianni did not know the name of the servant girl, nor did he wonder what was in those dark doorways, nor was he inclined to consider the life of the servant girl. It was not that he had other things on his mind. In truth, his mind was often like a large empty bowl. His tutors attempted to fill this bowl each day, but, to their endless frustration, the Prince had a way of emptying it with astonishing speed.

Three knocks rapped on the heavy oaken door.

"Your Royal Highness, Heir to the Throne of Corona, Prince Gianni. It is I, Tutor of Diplomacy. It is time for—"

"Oh, enter, enter," Prince Gianni said. "Get on with it."

The first king of Corona was what you might expect a king should be: strong, wise, and brave—in all ways a leader. But the present king, Guido, was the twelfth king of Corona, and whatever strength and wisdom and bravery his ancestors might have had, those qualities had been diluted over the years, so that King Guido was neither particularly strong, nor terribly wise, and certainly not brave. His eldest son, Prince Gianni, was like his father in many ways: weak, empty-headed, and cowardly.

On the other hand, there was Prince Vito, at eleven the youngest in the royal family, who had inherited some of those long-lost kingly genes. He was a sturdy, robust boy, broad-shouldered and hardy, with steel-gray eyes and a chocolate mane of hair—an imposing figure. His nimble mind could absorb the most complicated information, and as for bravery, there was nothing yet that Prince Vito feared. Prince Vito might have seemed better suited to be the future king than his brother, Prince Gianni, but Prince Vito was the third-born child, and the second boy, the "spare heir," and in the long history of the kings of Corona, no spare had ever reached the throne.

There was also an aggressiveness about Prince Vito that, if you were a peasant whose life was ruled by someone like Vito, you might fear. Prince Vito enjoyed confrontation. He relished giving orders. He expected people to obey him, and he believed that those who disobeyed him deserved punishment, swift and fierce.

While his brother, Prince Gianni, was being

tutored on the floor above, Prince Vito was preparing for a fencing lesson. With him was the Dresser of Prince Vito, an elderly man who had served in the royal household his entire life, rising from cook's helper, to stable boy, to assistant-to-the-assistant-to-the-Dresser of the second prince, until at last he had reached this high position.

"Your Royal Highness, the Second Prince—" he said.

Prince Vito reeled. "Do not ever—do you hear me?—do not ever say "Second Prince" again."

"But Your Royal Highness—sir—Prince Vito of Corona—it is the official and proper address—"

"Not any longer," Prince Vito declared. "I hereby abolish it. I hereby forbid it!"

"Yes, sir, Prince, sir—"

Minutes later, the Dresser of Prince Vito, so intent on smoothing a wrinkle from the cuff of the Prince's fencing trousers, forgot, and said, "Your Royal Highness, the Second Prince—"

"Out! Out!" Prince Vito ordered. "To the

stables! I command it. Send me another dresser!"

Prince Vito believed strongly in two principles. The first was that one must not tolerate insubordination, for it led to a weak kingdom. The second principle was that there was an order in the world: there was royalty, and there was the rest of humanity, and always the distinction between the two should be quite clear.

It would be wonderful to say that Princess Fabrizia was the strongest, wisest, bravest, and kindest of all the King's children, but alas she was frail and foolish and, above all else, afraid of every little thing. Pampered and petted from the day she was born, the Princess had become a spoiled, silly twelve-year-old.

She had inherited her mother's auburn curls and violet eyes, and her skin was like that of a perfect, pale pink rose petal. It was easy to see why she was so pampered from the time she was a babe, why she was so protected and cosseted and swooned over. Although there are some children who thrive with such adoration,

Princess Fabrizia had instead become *insufferable.*

On this summer day, as Princess Fabrizia lifted her silver goblet of milk, sweetened with chocolate, to her lips, a stream spilled onto her lavender organza gown. "*Wahh! Anghh!*" A prolonged fit of terrifying intensity ensued: sobbing, gasping, wailing, which nothing could comfort. Maids hustled to and fro, dabbing, patting, mopping. "*Wahh!*"

In the courtyard below, a young servant girl stood beside the stable boy. They looked up at the source of the deafening wails.

"What do you think?" the boy asked. "Does she see a fly?"

"Or maybe," suggested the girl, "the Princess, she spies a dot of dust in the air?"

꩜ 4 ꩜

The Peasants

In the woods, Pia held the leather pouch. The leather was fine and soft, and she feared soiling it with her dirty hands. "Here," she said to Enzio, "hold this—carefully—by the cord." She wiped her hands on the rough cloth of her skirt. "Now, let me see it."

Enzio dutifully handed the pouch back to Pia, relieved not to have the responsibility of it. Pia examined the King's seal on one side of the pouch. Intricate layers of golden thread outlined a shield. In each of the four corners of the shield was an emblem, also woven with golden thread. Three of these emblems Pia could readily identify: a castle, a crown, and a tree.

'What's this fourth thing?" she asked Enzio.

Everyone, Pia and Enzio included, was familiar with the King's seal. It was stamped on official proclamations posted throughout the village; it was emblazoned on sacks of wheat and corn, on flags, and on the red cloaks of the King's Men. Pia and Enzio, however, had never looked that closely at each image.

"A carrot?" Enzio suggested.

Pia scoffed. "Never! An eel? Maybe a worm—"

"For a king? Never would he have a worm on his seal!"

"True," agreed Pia. She carefully assessed the weight of the pouch, which fit comfortably in her hands. "Not too heavy. It jingles."

"Coins? Gold coins?"

"Maybe. Wait. Listen—" The steady beat of hooves sounded again on the path.

"Coming back," Enzio said. "Get down."

Through the thicket, they saw two of the King's Men racing along the path, returning from the direction they had gone. Trailing them was a lone King's Man, riding slowly, halting here and there.

"He looks for something," Pia whispered.

Enzio snatched the pouch from her hands and shoved it under a pile of leaves.

5

The King and Queen

King Guido and Queen Gabriella, dressed in their golden robes and golden crowns, were sitting on their thrones. Standing before them was the Minister of the Daily Schedule, droning on about their appointments for the day.

The Minister of the Daily Schedule was a short, round, pudgy fellow with an absurd black mustache which curled upward at the ends, lending him the appearance of perpetually grinning. His bulging stomach strained at the buttons of his green silk waistcoat; his chubby thighs rippled beneath his blue silk trousers; and his tiny feet in their pointed purple shoes looked much too small to hold up this round fellow. His voice sounded like the low drone of a cloud of locusts.

He had already outlined the upcoming meetings with the Minister of Meals, the Minister of Ceremony, and the Mistress of Housekeeping, and now he was buzzing on about the meeting with the Minister of Village Relations. "At two o'clock, the minister will give his monthly accounting of the economics and social stability of—"

The King yawned. "Oh, bother," he said. "Bother, bother, bother." He tugged at the sleeves of his golden robe. "This thing is so itchy."

The Queen patted his hand. "Now, now, Guidie," she soothed. While the minister continued talking, her eyes focused on the stained glass windows above his head. The sun, streaming through them, cast rays of yellow and green and blue and lilac across the floor in such a charming way.

Queen Gabriella was a striking woman, tall and slender, with a halo of auburn tresses and deep, penetrating violet eyes that made many visitors gasp and lower their own, inferior eyes. In public she always deferred to the King, remaining soft-spoken and gracious. Her litany of phrases on official occasions included "How nice to meet you" and "How very nice to meet you" and "Thank you for coming" and "Thank you *so very much* for coming."

Such insignificant things—a spotted gown, a sour melon, drooping flowers—were brought to her attention. *Can no one around here use his brain*? she wondered. *Does no one think of larger things?* For the Queen, these larger things were many and varied, and they occupied her mind during the trivial ceremonies and feasts and meetings. What did the ocean look like? The jungle? A lion? What would it be like to wander freely again, wherever she might choose? What is it like to create music—to write the notes, to hear them in your head before a musical instrument brings them to the air? At times the Queen's mind also roamed sadder passageways: What had become of her parents and siblings, long ago left behind in another kingdom?

King Guido, too, let his mind wander during the endless official occasions, but his mind wandered to other realms. He hoped he would not see another snake in the garden. Snakes terrified him. He wished his robes did not itch and that he could wander around in his soft nightshirt. He wished he did not have to walk up and down all those cold stone steps from his bedchamber to the throne room. He hoped he would not have to go hunting with today's visitors. His bottom still hurt from yesterday's ride.

Now, in the throne room, the Minister of the Daily Schedule, winding down, said, "And finally, the Minister of Defense will report on the thief."

"Thief?" the King said. "What thief?"

"Thief?" echoed the Queen.

The minister shuffled his papers and mopped his brow with his burgundy handkerchief. He'd been afraid they would take notice of that word *thief*. That is why he'd left it to the end, when he hoped they would be so inattentive or so anxious for him to finish that they would not hear that one word.

The King's hand fluttered on his knee. "Did you say *thief?*"

"Have we misheard you?" asked the Queen.

"Shall I leave it to the Minister of Defense to explain?" the minister suggested.

"But you said *thief.*"

"Surely not *here,*" the Queen said. "You're not talking about a thief in *our* kingdom?"

"I do not have the information," the minister said. "The Minister of Defense will explain, I am sure." And with that, he hastily bowed and retreated, leaving the King and Queen sitting on their thrones, looking at each other, both of them thinking, *Thief?*

The King could not remember the last time the word *thief* had been used. Had it ever been used in his lifetime? And if it had not been used, how did he know what it meant?

Queen Gabriella read his mind. "From stories we know of thieves. The Wordsmith has talked of them—"

"Terrible things, thieves, always dashing about stealing things that don't belong to them."

"But we have no thieves in *our* kingdom, Guidie. Surely?"

"Never!" sputtered the King. "Never! Terrible things, those thieves."

And yet, the Queen wondered, *why* did they not have thieves? She climbed the stone steps to her bedchamber, stopping at a window on the landing. Below her spread the interior courtyard, bustling with servants and rimmed with flowers, birds diving here and there. Through the open main gate of the castle, more lush gardens unfurled. One path led to the King's "folly," the hermit's cottage.

Beyond loomed the stone wall, and stretching below was the grand and familiar vista of rolling green hills and pastures dotted with wildflowers. At the base of the hills wound the beautiful Winono River, silvery blue in the sunlight, and on the far banks of the river curled the village. The village was a sprawling array of low stone houses with red-tiled roofs, the marketplace with its colorful banners of blue and red and gold, and at the far edges, rows of timber huts with thatched roofs.

From her perch on the landing, the Queen could survey the entire small Kingdom of Corona. She contemplated the peasants she had met in her twice-yearly excursions to the village. Their faces were always well-scrubbed, and although their clothes were of rough cloth and ill-fitting, they were clean. The children beamed up at her and the King, offering bouquets of wildflowers plucked from the meadows. The villagers seemed a loyal and placid lot. How could there be a thief among them?

King Guido stood in the center of the throne room, still stunned by the mention of that word *thief*. He was not thinking of the peasants in the village. Instead, he was preoccupied with one single thought: *What has been stolen?* To his First Servant, the King commanded, "Bring me the Minister of Inventory!"

"The Minister of Inventory of what?" the servant inquired. "Of Food? Of Clothing? Of

Horses? Of Armor? Of Silver? Of Gold? Of—"

"Oh, bother!" said the King. "Bring all of them, all the Ministers of Inventory!"

6

An Encounter

Pia was a slender girl with large, round dark eyes and thick black lashes, curly black hair, long legs, and an easy, graceful way of moving. In many ways she was unlike other peasants in the village, who tended to be sturdy and stocky and who strode about purposefully and with little grace. Pia did not know how old she was. Her master said twelve; an old woman down the lane said thirteen.

The villagers called her "the eagle girl," for her alert look and her confidence, and although she often dreamed of flying, she was not one to be easily labeled. She could be feisty, if challenged, but she could also be silent, withholding her temper. There was a girlishness in her open joy at the smallest of pleasures: a bird sailing through the sky, cool river water, a piece of red cloth found in the market. At the same time, there could be a mature air about her: she avoided self-pity, respected others' feelings, and looked after her brother.

Pia did not often dwell on daily challenges, preferring to imagine where she and Enzio had come from and what might become of them. In this was hope and possibility, although nothing in her life thus far gave her reason to believe things could change—nothing, that is, except the *thing* inside her that made her Pia.

Pia had no recollection of her parents, and only a dim memory of a tall, slim figure she had called Grandpapa. She occasionally glimpsed one early memory, of a dark ride beneath a blanket in a creaky wagon on a moonlit night, the taste of salt on her tongue, the smell of garlic in the air, whispers around her, and someone saying, "*Bellissima, bellissima*," over and over. She did not recall Enzio being in that wagon, but all subsequent memories included him, along with the understanding that this was her brother, and that she was the older one and obliged to take care of him.

Enzio was lean and loose-jointed, tall for his age (ten? eleven?), with an angular but agreeable face framed by wavy, tangled brown hair that glimmered in the summer with streaks of gold. His long, slim fingers, calloused with work, were, like his face, ruddy from the sun. Enzio's open, trusting look was at odds with his inner caution when Pia was out of his sight.

Enzio's earliest memory was of Pia bandaging his knee in the dark, dirt-floored hut that belonged to their master. He couldn't recall a mother or father, only Pia, always there by his side. Pia had told him that they had not always lived with the master, that they had been brought there, but when or by whom, she did not know.

Often the two of them imagined that they had come from someplace vastly different, a special place, and one day they would find their way back again, and they would find parents and grandparents and aunts and uncles and cousins. These shared dreams alternated with their individual ones. Enzio dreamed of plentiful food, of traveling down the river on a raft, and most often, of riding white horses through the meadows.

"On a horse, Pia, I could go anywhere, anywhere!"

Pia's dreams included entering the castle gates, for she longed to see what was inside; and she dreamed of touching the hand of someone related to her, someone other than Enzio, to know that she and he were not alone in this world. Her most frequent, and most implausible, dream was of flying, of feeling she could lift off and move about the world at her whim.

On this day, however, they crouched in the thicket near the river, watching one of the King's Men on his horse, ambling down the path. He stopped here and there, peering into the leaves.

"Searching," Enzio whispered.

"For the pouch," Pia said.

Enzio's eyes flickered to the pile of leaves

under which he had stashed the leather pouch emblazoned with the King's seal. "Maybe there's a reward?"

"For peasants? Not probably."

"Halt!" shouted the King's Man. "Come out!" He drew his sword, aiming it in their direction.

Pia and Enzio stood. "It is only us," Enzio said. "Peasants."

"Come out—slowly," ordered the King's Man.

Pia and Enzio emerged from the thicket, lowering their gaze, as they had been taught to do. They could see the muscled legs of the horse, the polished black boots of the rider, and the lower edge of his red cloak. They could smell the horse's sweat.

"Look up! Let me see your scruffy faces."

They raised their heads, taking in the gleaming chocolate horse and the tall, sturdy man, with his heavy-lidded eyes and prominent nose, the full sweep of his red cloak sparkling with gold medallions and the crest of the King over his heart.

"What are you doing here?" he demanded.

Pia was bursting to speak, but looked to Enzio, for she had been taught that a soldier would expect a reply from a boy, not from a girl.

"Fetching water from the river," Enzio said.

"In the bushes?"

"And berries," Enzio added. "For the master."

"And who is your master?"

"Master Pangini."

"I know him, a stern one, likes to think he is a big man." The King's Man replaced his sword in its sheath, but he did not dismount. From on high, he asked, "Have you seen anyone go by?"

Pia leaned against Enzio, her sign that he should be careful with his words.

"One rider on a black horse," Enzio said, "followed by the King's Men, and then two of the King's Men coming back this way."

The soldier glared at them, weighing Enzio's words. "What else?"

"That's all," Enzio said. "Were you chasing

him—the rider on the black horse?"

The soldier shifted in his saddle, looking back the way he had come. "You did not find anything? The rider did not drop anything or cast anything aside?"

Pia and Enzio had learned, from their life with the gruff Master Pangini, that the truth was sometimes to be coveted, like a treasure. If they had known and respected the soldier, they might have offered him their gift of truth, but they were wary of him. Instinctively, they presented the man their open, eager expressions.

"Like what?" Enzio said. "You want us to look for you?"

"If you should find an object that . . . does not belong to you, that looks . . . important, what would you do with it?"

Pia and Enzio looked at each other and shrugged. "What *should* we do with it?" Enzio said.

The King's Man wrinkled his brow and stared at them, as if he would bore a hole in their foreheads with his gaze. "You would not keep it?"

"No," Enzio said. "Never!"

"For that would be stealing," the King's Man said.

Enzio and Pia remained silent.

"If you should find anything, go to the old woman Ferrelli—you know her?"

"Everyone knows her," Enzio replied.

"Good," the King's Man said. "You go to her with the . . . object, and she will know what to do."

"I hope we find it!" Enzio said. "Is it very important?"

"It is . . . significant. Remember my words." And with that, the King's Man galloped off in the direction of the castle.

Pia glanced back at the thicket. "Significant," she said.

Enzio nodded sagely. "Significant!"

7

The Royal Riders

Prince Gianni, heir to the throne, and Prince Vito, the spare, were mounted on their white horses, waiting for Princess Fabrizia. Circling them were nine King's Men who would serve as guards and escorts. Two stable boys were attempting to assist the Princess up the portable wooden steps and into her saddle.

"Take care!" ordered the Princess. "It's a new gown and a new cloak."

Sitting upright and rigid on his horse, Prince Gianni gazed out across the meadow. "Another day, another ride," he murmured.

Prince Vito's horse was stamping and snorting, echoing the younger Prince's own impatience. Prince Vito wanted to tear across the fields, race across the meadow and on into the woods, but he knew that with the Princess accompanying them, it would be a slow, tame ride.

From a window, the Queen observed her children with a sudden rush of maternal pride. *How regal they look.* Normally she was frank in her assessment of her children's weaknesses. She was well aware of Prince Gianni's sullenness and his empty head; she was not blind to Prince Vito's aggressiveness; and she was often embarrassed by the Princess's tantrums. But on this sunny day, as she watched them ride off on their white horses, she felt only tenderness and a ripple of protective wariness. This puzzled her, as she was rarely wary and never fearful. What had come over her? Perhaps it was that word *thief*, still floating in her mind.

The King, meanwhile, was in his dressing chamber, lying on a brocade divan, suffering through the First Dresser's suggestions as to which trousers and which royal jacket would be suitable for the day's appointments.

"May I recommend this one?" inquired the

Dresser, holding forth a cream silk jacket emblazoned with the King's crest and embellished with heavy gold braiding around the cuffs and lapels.

"Too scratchy," the King said.

"Then possibly this one?"

"I'm weary of blue."

Two timid raps sounded at the door.

"Oh, bother," the King said. "Who now? Enter. Enter!"

When the door opened, a stream of men and women, forty-seven in number, entered, all dressed in the black-and-red cloaks of the royal staff.

"What's this?" the King grumbled. "Who are all of you? What do you want?"

One of them answered, "We are the Ministers of Inventory. You summoned us."

"*Hrmph.*"

"We are all here, except for the Minister of Inventory of Vegetables, because he is ill today, I am sorry to report."

"I hardly think his absence will be important," mumbled the King. "Very well, then, I want to know what is missing."

"Missing, sire?"

"Yes, missing. Which of you is missing something from your inventory?"

The ministers looked from one to another. A short, gray-haired man at the back said, "Excuse us, sire, but if you want an up-to-date accounting, we will each have to do an inventory—"

"Ach! Isn't that what you *do*? Don't you make inventories?"

The gray-haired man cleared his throat. "Yes, sire, but not every day."

"Well, when, then? When was the last time you took inventory?"

Again the ministers looked from one to another, each hoping someone else would speak. A wiry, pale man nearest the King said, "Speaking for myself, and I am the Minister of Inventory of Oats, my last full inventory was two weeks past."

"Two *weeks?*" said the King. "So you would not be able to tell me if anything was missing from, say, this week?"

"Missing, sire?"

"Missing! Something is missing!"

"What, sire?"

Two purple veins bulged on the King's forehead. "If I knew what, I would not have summoned you! I want to know what is missing, and I want to know it by darkness."

"Tonight?"

"Tonight! Now, away, all of you, and I want a full reporting by darkness. Tonight!"

The ministers retreated, looking anxious. The King let his head fall back against the divan. He was exhausted. He did not like confrontation. He did not like to give orders. He wanted to take a nap.

8

The Hermitage

From time to time, when the King was feeling burdened, he made his way through the main castle gate and down the gentle slope toward a simple stone building. He first had to wind through the outer gardens, lush and charming, with pebbled paths curling between clipped box hedges and masses of lavender, which tickled his ankles.

On a recent walk, he had stopped to rest on a curved granite bench, inhaling the sweet aromas and admiring a richly golden finch which perched in a nearby bush. "Perhaps you are the king of birds," the King said aloud. The bird cocked its head. "And you, like me, are resting here, before you must go back to ruling your kingdom, hmm?" The bird appeared to be listening, and this had amused the King. He was enjoying an unusual feeling of calm when he saw a flicker of movement on the edge of the stone path, off to his right. A snake. A long, thick, black snake slithering along. The King jumped up, clasping his fists against his chest and stomping his foot on the ground. "Go! Go! Begone!" he ordered. The goldfinch darted from its perch and flew off. The snake stopped. "Begone!" insisted the King.

Instead of fleeing, the snake slid along the path in the direction of the King. Baffled and terrified by the snake's persistence, the King had ran off, stumbling down the path, peeking behind him to see if the snake was pursuing him. It was. The King fled beneath trellises overrun with roses, darted between sculpted bushes, and ran until he reached the hermitage at the bottom of the hill.

Today, however, with thoughts of a thief in his head, the King made his way quickly through the gardens, relieved that there was no sign of the snake. He composed himself before knocking at the gray wooden door. The hermitage was a simple, square building. The stones that composed its walls had been hauled from the river below, and even on a sunny, warm day like this, the scent of river arose from these walls.

The King heard the latch release, and as the door swung inward, a rush of cool air greeted him. He blinked in the darkness of the entryway, able to discern only the familiar outline of the hermit.

9

The Pouch

Pia and Enzio stood in the thicket near the river. The air was still and quiet, interrupted only by the occasional *terrip, terrip* of crickets. The sister and brother were shaded on one side by a bank of tall oak trees. On the other side the wild grass stretched to the riverbank, and overhead sprawled a clear blue sky with one fleecy cloud which, to Pia, resembled a cauliflower.

Cupped in Pia's hands was the leather pouch emblazoned with the King's seal. "We should see what's inside," she said.

Enzio agreed.

"There is nothing wrong with looking," Pia said.

"No, nothing wrong about that."

"Only natural to look."

"Anyone would do it."

Pia smoothed the leather. "If we are to give this to the old woman Ferrelli, we should at least know what we are giving her, shouldn't we?"

"Yes. We should."

Pia offered the pouch to Enzio. "Do you want to—"

Enzio took a step backward. "No. You."

"Whatever is inside—we couldn't damage it, could we?"

Enzio thought for a moment. "It might be delicate."

Pia again assessed the bulk of it in her hands. "Doesn't feel delicate."

"Open it."

"Now?"

"Now."

They moved farther back into the woods. When Enzio had brushed the ground clear of leaves, they kneeled. Holding the pouch firmly in one hand, Pia slid its contents into the open palm of her other hand. They bent close to the objects: two small pieces of red coral; a pair of golden medallions; a lock of black hair tied with a purple ribbon; and a small, rolled piece of parchment on which were written, in curling black script, words which they could not read.

Enzio was most interested in the identical medallions. On one side of each was the King's seal, and on the other side was an intricate embossed design which resembled a maze or a convoluted flower. Pia examined the pieces of coral. Each was the familiar shape of a *corno*, a horn-shaped token of good luck. These were common enough amulets—many villagers wore similar ones to ward off the *malocchio*, the evil eye—but those the villagers wore were carved from wood. Only once had Pia seen a coral one. The two in her hand were more finely crafted and of a deeper, purer coral than the one she had seen. Pia had heard villagers talk of golden *cornos*, too, which only royalty possessed.

Pia held the lock of hair lightly between her fingers, feeling its soft texture. She stroked the hair and its ribbon as she studied the script on the parchment.

"Wonder what it says, Enzio."

"Anything else on there? On the back?"

"No. Nothing."

Indicating the medallions, Enzio said, "These, at least, must be valuable. Gold!"

"But what is the connection, do you think? *Cornos*, medallions, a lock of hair, and a piece of paper with words?"

"Maybe the words explain, or maybe there is no connection," Enzio said. "Maybe they are just things that got stuck in this pouch."

"And why would someone want to steal it?"

"The gold," Enzio said. "Think how much these must be worth!"

"So, we are supposed to take this to the old woman Ferrelli, yes?"

"That's what the King's Man said."

"And if we don't—"

"He said it would be stealing."

Pia curled the purple ribbon around her finger. "But right now—right now—we are only *finding*, yes?"

Enzio studied Pia's face, reading her thoughts. "Yes," he agreed. "We are only *finding* something on the path."

"And the King's Man did not say *when* we should take whatever we found to the old woman Ferrelli, did he?"

"No, he did not."

"So," Pia urged, "we do not have to take it to her instantly?"

Enzio smiled. "He didn't say anything about *instantly*."

ൠ 10 ൠ

The Hermit

The hermit gestured to a straw mat, and the King took his usual place, settling himself cross-legged on the floor. The hermit sat across from the King on a similar straw mat. Neither had yet spoken, for this was the way of the hermitage: silence first.

It had been the King's desire to acquire the hermit, and although the King knew that others referred to this as his "folly," he did not mind. A king should be allowed his follies. His interest in his own personal hermit had first arisen when Count Volumnia had visited. The Count was a great traveler and was fond of reporting his discoveries, most of which revolved around the latest acquisitions of other noblemen. During his visit with the King, the Count mentioned that among the intriguing things he had discovered recently was a "most wonderful novelty" which he had found on the grounds of a grand villa. The villa's owner had built an outlying cottage and had installed therein a hermit.

"But why?" asked the King.

"Because," replied the Count, "he wanted a muse."

"But—a hermit?"

"The hermit spends all day, each and every day, contemplating the universe. Spiritual matters. Inspirational matters. A great deal of time was spent searching for the right hermit."

"But why—how—of what benefit is this to the owner of the villa?" asked the King.

"The hermit's job—his purpose—is to inspire his master, to offer him enlightenment and wisdom."

"Ah," said the King. "Enlightenment. Wisdom."

Although the King did not have any strong

desire for enlightenment or wisdom, he wondered if he should keep up with the times and install his own hermit on the castle grounds. The more he thought about this idea, the more it took hold in his mind, and soon a dozen of the King's Men were sent out to scour the countryside for the perfect hermit.

After several months, when the King was becoming aggravated by the slowness of the search, a hermit was brought to him. The King's Man who ushered the hermit into the King's quarters said, "He is the perfect hermit. He is enlightened. He is wise."

"And how do you know this?" the King asked.

"Everyone says so."

"Everyone?"

"Everyone."

And so the King had met the hermit, a tall, thin man with thick gray hair and round, soft, dark eyes. He had a slow and gentle manner, and when the King spoke to him, the hermit's replies were hushed. The King outlined his proposal: he would build a small house for the hermit on the castle grounds, and the hermit would live there, with no duties except to contemplate the universe and share his wisdom with the King.

"I have a few family obligations," the hermit said.

This was not welcome news. The King didn't want any hangers-on—no wives or children or elderly parents. There were enough people in the castle already. Too many! He wanted only the gentle hermit. When the hermit explained his family obligations, the King was glad that with some simple arrangements those responsibilities could be taken care of, and the hermit—alone—would be willing and able to serve as the King's personal hermit.

"A *what?*" the Queen had said, when the King informed her of his decision to install the hermit on the grounds. "Did you say—a *hermit?* Have I heard you correctly?"

"Yes, yes, a hermit, a counsel of enlightenment and wisdom."

The Queen raised her eyebrows, but she was reluctant to question the King because he seemed determined to have his way. Besides, she was curious about the sort of enlightenment and wisdom that the hermit might bring. "Wonderful, Guidie! I will be eager to meet your hermit."

"Ahem," murmured the King. "Remember, he is *my* hermit. You probably won't see much of him."

"Oh," the Queen said, disappointed. "Of course, Guidie."

And so the stone house was built and the hermit arrived. He had now been in his silent stone enclave for nearly a decade.

The King and the hermit sat across from each other in the soundless space of the hermitage for some time. At last the King spoke.

"Hermit? Today we have learned that a thief has been in our midst."

The hermit nodded.

"A *thief!* We don't have thieves in our kingdom! Never have I heard of such a thing. You can imagine how troubling this news is."

Again the hermit nodded.

The King explained about the Minister of Defense's vague report of a black-cloaked figure racing through the courtyard clutching a sack, mounting a black horse, and fleeing. The King also said that he had ordered inventories to see what might have been stolen, and he had bid his men find the thief. Punctuating his account were the hermit's nods.

During his first few visits with the hermit, these silent nods had unnerved the King, but over time he had come to appreciate the soft gestures of the old man. Here was someone who would not argue with him, would not pester him with questions. The hermit would listen, mute, without judgment and, when he was ready, he would offer a few well-chosen words. Those few words, the King assumed, were wisdom or enlightenment, and he felt privileged and grateful that he alone was the recipient of the wise and enlightened words of his own personal hermit.

On this day, after the King had presented his tale of the thief, the hermit clasped his hands together and closed his eyes, as he usually did before offering his words. The King waited, not overly anxious for the hermit to speak, for he enjoyed the quiet comfort of this place, and he knew that once the hermit spoke it would be time for the King to leave, to return to the bustle of the castle, to the obligations and duties that awaited him.

When the hermit finally spoke, it was in his usual gentle, measured tones. "A thief," he said, "wants what he does not have."

The King let these words cross the space between him and the hermit and enter his mind. "A thief," he repeated, "wants what he does not have." It sounded very wise.

꩜ 11 ꩜

Wisdom

The Queen could always tell when the King had visited the hermit, for he would be, for a short time, calmer than usual, not straining at his restrictive clothing, not complaining or yawning. She would find him sitting mute on his throne, his hands folded one atop the other, gazing placidly around the room.

On this late afternoon, when the castle was still buzzing with word of the thief, the Queen, passing the throne room, spotted the King resting comfortably on his throne. *Ah*, she thought, *so he has been to see the hermit*. She entered the room quietly, gliding slowly across the cool marble floor until she reached him.

"Guidie?"

"*Mm?*"

"Are you well, Guidie?"

The King nodded, in much the same manner as the hermit: slowly, calmly. The Queen settled herself beside him on her own throne and waited. She knew that he would soon offer a pronouncement, but it would not come if she pestered him with questions. She had learned this over time. The Queen folded her hands like the King and serenely contemplated the room, noting the amber light, flecked with violet, which streamed through the stained glass windows and formed a delicate light pool on a square of marble tile.

"A thief," the King said solemnly, "wants what he does not have."

What he said made perfect sense, but the Queen was annoyed that she hadn't thought of this herself. On further reflection, she was sure she *had known* such a thought, but merely had never put it into words. She was also quite sure that the King's pronouncement came from the hermit because she knew the King well, and she knew that he did not make such clear observations on his own.

"That's very profound, Guidie," she said, aware that she was jealous of the King's access to his personal hermit. Perhaps, she thought (and not for the first time), she should acquire her own hermit.

"And so," the King continued, "we must find out what the thief does not have."

"But, Guidie, we do not know who the thief is, do we?"

The King glanced at her, and in that glance the Queen saw displeasure. He was emerging from the hermit-induced calm, and she knew that soon he would be his usual, irritable, self.

"Then we must find out," the King said, "who does not have something, and then we shall find the thief."

The Queen wanted to jump up from her gilded throne and shout, "That is absurd! Ludicrous! Everyone does not have *something*!" Instead, she composed herself. She said, "Yes, Guidie, dear," and, smiling at him, she rose.

Mustering all her self-control, she drifted calmly away. Once outside the chamber, she pressed both hands over her mouth to muffle an exasperated groan.

The three royal riders and their nine guards rode slowly back up the hill to the castle. Prince Gianni, the eldest, said, "I hope we are not expected to be on duty tonight."

Princess Fabrizia swished her handkerchief at a pesky fly. "But Gianni, we are on duty, for we have visitors: Count Volumnia—"

"No!" said Prince Vito. "Not the obsequious Count and his obsequious wife?" Vito was prickly enough already, having plodded along on the slow, dull ride, when all he had wanted to do was race across the fields, leap the stream, and ride as hard and as fast as he could.

"Obsequious?" Prince Gianni hated when his younger brother used words like *obsequious*, because he did not know what they meant. Where had his brother learned that word? Had he, Gianni, learned the word and forgotten it?

“*Obsequious* means “fawning,”” Prince Vito said. “It’s that awful thing the Count does—‘Oh, noble King Guido,” and “Oh, most beauteous Queen Gabriella.” Makes me want to throw a cabbage at him.”

Princess Fabrizia giggled. “Vito, that isn’t princely.”

In response, Prince Vito slapped his horse with his whip and took off, leaving his sister and brother coughing in his dust. Prince Vito charged up the crest of the hill toward the exterior gates, with three of the King’s Men in pursuit, for the King’s Men’s orders were to never let any of the children out of their sight. Vito rode hard through the gates and veered sharply to the right, knowing that, at least briefly, he *would* be out of their sight and that they would be vexed and anxious as a result.

Prince Vito halted behind the hermitage. From inside, a shadow crossed the narrow opening in the wall, a bare window draped with oilcloth. Prince Vito had never had any particular interest in the hermit. If anything, he regarded the hermit—an old, shuffling man rarely seen outside—with scorn. Such a preposterous figure, Prince Vito thought. But on this day, as he sat on his horse, hiding from the King's Men, Prince Vito was curious. *What does that hermit do all day?*

A mottled hand drew back the oilcloth, and the hermit gazed directly at the Prince. He did not smile or bow, as was the custom and the duty of underlings; he simply stood there watching with his dark, peaceful eyes. But there was something more in his look, something penetrating and unsettling.

The Prince was about to order the old man to bow, when he heard the oncoming hoof-beats of the King's riders. Prince Vito brought his whip down hard on his horse and raced off, forgetting the hermit.

12

The Old Woman

Master Pangini shook his whip at Pia and Enzio. "You dirty beetles, where have you been? Dallying about? Girl, where is my food? Boy, get to the stall and take over for Rocco so he can have his meal. You idle, lazy turnips."

Pia snatched the bread from its bin, lit the fire, and whirled a spoon through the stew she had cooked the day before. Master Pangini's tantrums did not ruffle her. It was his blustery way, full of noise and flutter, signifying nothing. Often, during his tirades, Pia would imagine herself lifting into the air, flying out the door and over rooftops, swooping over the river, dipping and diving, and riding a current up the hill to the Castle Corona.

Today, though, Pia's mind was occupied with other things as she swirled Master Pangini's meal together. She and Enzio had hidden the pouch high in a gnarled oak tree. It was a spot they had used before: a solid, bowl-shaped indentation where a sturdy limb met the trunk. The two branches below this formed a firm platform on which they had spent many stolen hours imagining other lives for themselves.

Pia was usually the instigator of their imagined scenarios. "Enzio," she might say, "who knows where we might have come from? We might have come from a royal household that was set upon by bandits, and our parents had to give us away for our safekeeping."

Enzio, then, was able to spin the scene further. "And the first person she gave us to was probably a kind and gentle woman, don't you think?"

"But the woman . . . she fell over a cliff—"

"When she was watching the goats—"

"Oh, yes, I like goats. That's good, Enzio. And then the wretched Pangini came along and snatched us up—"

"And he was a snarly, gruff man—"

"A very large, round, snarly, gruff man—"

On they would go, creating their possible former lives and landing themselves with the gruff Pangini. If they had time, they would continue with what-happens-next. "Enzio, one day our former family will find us, and we will return to the castle—"

"Where we shall ride white horses and eat fine foods . . ."

During their trek back to Pangini's hovel, these images stayed with them, making it easier to resume their chores and endure the meagerness of life with Pangini.

As Pia stirred Pangini's stew, she was hoping the pouch, hidden in the tree-bowl, would be secure until she and Enzio could decide what to do with it. Pia felt the itch of curiosity. Who owned the contents of the pouch? Who had stolen it? Why was it stolen?

"Food!" demanded Master Pangini. "You

think I can work all day without food?"

Pia set the bowl of stew before him, along with thick slices of bread and a mug of ale. She stepped back, hoping there would be scraps left for her and Enzio to eat, but knowing that her master's appetite was enormous. She wondered how a man who did so little could require so much food. His version of work was to stroll back and forth in front of his market stall, snapping at his worker, Rocco. "Peel back those cabbages—who will buy them if they look rotten?" and "Pile the oranges, pile them! Don't lump them like that!" and "Careful of that cook's helper—he likes to stuff his pockets when you're not looking!"

Enzio raced down the dirt path to the marketplace, happy to be out of Master Pangini's sight, but sorry that Pia remained under the master's eye. It was a beautiful day: deep blue sky and a breeze spinning scents of fresh fruits and flowers through the air.

Rocco was leaning against the stall, chatting with a peasant girl. He was a short, stout young man, lazy but good-humored. Rocco handed his apron, with its deep pockets jingling with change, over to Enzio and winked at the girl.

Enzio savored this time at the stall, away from the master, watching the people come and go, listening to the lively gossip, greeting familiar faces. Villagers called him "antelope boy," for his lean, agile swiftness.

An old man greeted him that way now. "Antelope boy! You have melons today? Let me see what Pangini has in his fancy crates."

Enzio helped the old man select his melons. As he dropped them in the man's sack, he stopped short, for there at the far end of the stall was the old woman Ferrelli, draped in black, sniffing grapes. Enzio turned away from her, feeling suddenly guilty. *If you should find anything, go to the old woman Ferrelli*, the King's Man had said.

It was not unusual to see Signora Ferrelli at the stall, but on this day, Enzio sensed that she had come for another purpose, that she knew that he and Pia had found the pouch. He busied himself with stacking oranges, hoping the old woman would move on, but she did not, and at last she approached him with two large bunches of purple grapes in her hands.

"I'll have these," she said, fumbling in her coin purse. Her voice was raspy, like a rusted saw scraping against metal. "You are well, antelope boy?"

"Yes, Signora Ferrelli, and you?"

Signora Ferrelli shrugged. "I am an old woman. I see too much. I hear too much."

Enzio slipped the grapes into her sack, then handed her coins back to her, refusing payment. "People trust you," he said.

"Eh? Trust me?" She studied Enzio's face. "So they trust me. This is true."

"A good day to you," he said.

"Ah, that is no small thing. A good day to you, too."

"Cabbages?" called a peasant girl standing nearby. "Three cabbages?"

By the time he had helped the girl, the old woman Ferrelli had vanished, but Enzio's uneasy awareness of the stolen pouch had not.

13

Preparations

The King had been spared from entertaining visitors in the late afternoon, because their arrival had been delayed, and so he had indulged in a long nap. As he emerged from sleep, with the cool feel of the pillowcase on his cheek, the King was reluctant to leave his bed. His first waking thoughts were of the gentle hermit, but those thoughts led to the hermit's words: *A thief wants what he does not have*. Instantly, the King was grumpy. Now I have to sort out this thief business. *Why did this thief have to come along?* And then there were the impending visitors to consider, the Count and Countess Volumnia and their endless chattering.

While the King had napped, the Queen strolled through a peaceful spot: the hornbeam tunnel, a long, winding, cool green tunnel of hornbeam trees. The tunnel, formed by intertwining hornbeam birches arching overhead, was where she went to be comforted, for it was quiet and embracing, and it was where she was often inspired. She was lifted and ennobled by the presence of these ancient trees.

She was reminded here of her royal duties—not the mindless daily ones of attending to visitors, but those reflecting the symbolic stature of the King and Queen: to be above lowly concerns and to set an example of honor and grace. Midway down the path, her back straightened, and she moved with more poise, gliding along, listening to the warbling birds, appreciating the clean, crisp aroma of the trees.

At the end of the path, the Queen emerged feeling refreshed, but this was a fleeting sensation, for what greeted her was the sight of the polished black carriage of the Count and

Countess Volumnia nearing the castle entrance. Her spirits sagged. To erase the sight of her visitors, she shifted her gaze to the opposite direction and spotted the hermitage at the base of the hill. The Queen longed to race down the hill and through the door of the small stone enclave. She was irked that her presence there was forbidden.

Needing to boost her spirits, the Queen vowed to acquire her own hermit, with his—or her (yes, she thought, *maybe it should be a female hermit*)—own sheltered cloister, to which the Queen could escape and where she could receive wisdom and enlightenment. With that resolve, she made her way back up the hill to prepare to greet her visitors.

Prince Gianni, heir to the throne, leaned against his windowsill, absently viewing the courtyard, while the First Dresser to the First Prince was laying out the Prince's clothes for the evening. The Prince saw the Count's gleaming black carriage enter the castle grounds.

"Ugh," he murmured. "The Count arrives."

The Prince regarded the castle walls and the view through the gate: more gardens, a wall, the sloping meadow, the river like a sinuous snake winding its way below, and the red-tiled roofs of the village beyond. He felt a formless sensation of yearning—but yearning for what?

His younger brother, Prince Vito, stood atop a large wooden chest in his chambers, slashing at the air with his sword. "Take that! And that!" He conjured up fearsome enemies, enormous men swathed in black. "Take that!" He cut them down, one by one. Prince Vito leaped from the chest, arms akimbo. "I am Protector of the Realm!" he shouted.

Princess Fabrizia sat at her dressing table while her Lady-in-Waiting attended to her hair, twining blue silk ribbons among her curls. The Princess tilted her head this way and that.

"It does look lovely, doesn't it?"

"Yes, Princess Fabrizia, it does."

The Princess stroked the delicate lace on the cuffs of her sleeves. "And this lace, it is the finest?"

"Yes, Princess Fabrizia, it is."

The Princess regarded her lovely self in the looking glass and sighed. "But it's rather a shame, don't you think, that all this loveliness will be showered on the Count and Countess? No young princes in tow, no other young people at all."

"Yes, Princess Fabrizia, it is a shame."

The Princess sighed. "What is all this loveliness *for?*"

The Lady-in-Waiting did not reply, for she had occasionally wondered this herself, and she had no answer for the Princess.

14

The Count and Countess

Prince Vito waited in the receiving hall at the foot of the curved stone stairway. Dreading the descent of Count and Countess Volumnia, the Prince tapped his polished boot against the bottom step. He found himself thinking of the hermit, not sure why the old man had entered his thoughts. Prince Vito envied the man's freedom from constant visitors and official duties, but he cringed at the thought of the hermit's confined existence.

A rustling from above announced the Count and Countess Volumnia's preparations to descend the steps. There they were in all their splendor: ruffled and beribboned and rustling, two plump figures dressed in lime-green fabrics, the two of them resembling large, unripe pears.

The Countess's green velvet gown, festooned with blue and gold ribbons and ruffles, ballooned around her as she began the descent, her arm cradled in her husband's. Her purple satin shoes corralled her enormous feet, and on her head was a green-and-blue wimple protruding at either side of her forehead like two big horns. As she beamed down at Prince Vito, her fleshy cheeks reddening, she raised her free hand in a flourishing wave.

"Prince Vito!" she exclaimed. "How marvelous!"

The Count, straining to balance his own weighty self as well as his wife's bulk, was uttering various *oofs* and *mmphs*. An enormous brocaded green tunic trimmed with black velvet swept over his protruding belly and ended at his knees, revealing black tights and black velvet slippers below. On his head perched a black velvet cap trimmed with white feathers. *Oof. Mmph.*

When at last they reached the bottom of the stairs, the Count bowed low and the Countess curtsied (with some difficulty), their full attention on Prince Vito. The Count's words rushed out, accompanied by a full spray of spittle. "Prince Vito, what a great honor indeed, yes, there you are, how absolutely—"

Not to be outdone by her husband, the Countess simultaneously burst forth with her own plums. "Prince Vito, look at you, how you have grown, what a handsome—"

"—fortunate we are—"

"—young man you have become—"

Prince Vito smiled politely at the two green pears before him. He extended his hand to the Countess. "May I escort you into the chamber?"

"Oh, yes, of course," burbled the Countess. "How eager we are to see the King and Queen again, and the noble Prince Gianni and the most beautiful Princess Fabrizia—"

"Yes, yes," added the Count, as he followed the Prince and the Countess through the entryway to the reception chamber. “Yes, yes, our noble King, our gracious Queen, our—”

Chatter, chatter, chatter.

꩜ 15 ꩜

The Dirty Beetles

Master Pangini pushed his chair back from the table and belched. "Clean this up, you dirty, paltry beetle," he ordered. The master lumbered across the small room and through the curtained doorway which led to his bed, and within minutes, Pia heard his loud snoring.

"'Clean this up, you dirty beetle,'" she mocked. "I am *not* a dirty beetle." She spoke to the snoring sounds: "*You* are a dirty beetle."

She was sweeping the floors when Enzio returned from the market. "Pia! I saw the old woman Ferrelli—"

"At the market?"

"I think she knows—"

"What?"

"That we've found the pouch."

A shiny black beetle scurried past Pia's broom. *It's not dirty at all,* she thought. To Enzio she said, "That's not possible. You're imagining it."

"Maybe. Maybe not. She made me nervous."

"You didn't say anything, did you, about the pouch?"

"No, no. I said nothing."

"Good." She shifted her attention to the straw mats in the corner. "Help me with these." Once outside, as they beat the dust and dirt from the mats, Pia said, "We must be careful. We must find out more about that pouch."

"But how?" Enzio asked. He was suddenly afraid, and he regretted their discovery.

"People talk. We'll listen."

Enzio understood. He knew that the best talker of all, the best gossip in the village, was Franco, a barrel-bellied, blustering man who could not keep a word or a thought in his head. Everything came spewing out, like lava from a volcano. "Franco?" he said.

"Franco," Pia agreed.

As they were running down the lane, Enzio said, "The master will not be happy if we're not there when he wakes up—"

"*Poo!* He was snoring hard. He'll still be wallowing in that bed when we return."

Enzio could always count on Pia to reassure him. He loved that about his sister.

The blustering Franco could usually be found perched on a stool near the bakers' end of the market, darting his plump hands out now and then for a roll which had tumbled off a cart or a heel of bread which lay on the end of a stall. People stopped to listen to him gabble and to get the latest gossip which they, in turn, would carry off to share with others.

It was the middle of the afternoon, a time of day when most of the market's early shoppers were home preparing meals. It was a lazy time, when the stall workers sat on fat barrels and tilted their faces up to the sun, closing their eyes. Pia and Enzio spotted Franco on his stool, munching on a roll and spluttering a stream of words into the air at the same time. Surrounding him were several men and one woman, baskets over their arms, listening.

"Mmf, and you know the horse lady?" Franco was saying. "The one with the big teeth?"

One of the men made the sound of a horse neighing.

Franco chattered on. "Where did she get that pig? A big, full-grown pig? One day she has no pigs, and the next day she has a big fat pig."

"Humph," said another man.

"I hear she blackmailed old Lonzo," Franco said.

"No!" said the woman. "Lonzo?"

Franco shrugged. "What can I say? It's what I hear. I do not know if it is true."

It angered Pia when Franco did this. He would say anything that came into his head, and then he would say he didn't know if it was true, but he had already planted the seed of suspicion in people's minds. Now, for instance, she knew these peasants would go away and pass on the "news" about the horse lady, and they would forget to say that it might not be true, and people would treat the horse lady with distrust.

Pia and Enzio busied themselves pretending to examine loaves of bread as they listened to Franco natter away. He moved on from the horse lady to "the stick man" (a lean old fellow who slept in the streets) and then to "the goat girl" (so named because of her angular face), and on and on he went until, at last, they heard him mention the thief.

"Thief?" someone said.

"You haven't heard? Everyone knows," Franco said. "A castle thief, maybe more than one—of this I can't be sure—and valuable things were stolen: jewels, gold, silver. The King's Men are out searching."

More peasants had gathered around Franco now, attracted by the sudden buzzing of the others already there.

"*Thief?* Did he say *thief?*"

"Jewels? Stolen?"

"Gold? Silver?"

"But who—?"

Franco bit into another roll and chewed sloppily. "*Mmf.* The thief, I hear—and I do not know if this is true—but I hear he is from our own village. The King's Men will be swarming. Mark my words."

Circling in the air above Franco's head was a pale gray bird with faint tinges of yellow at its throat. Pia knew this bird and her mate, the brightly colored goldfinch, for they nested each year in a tree at this end of the market. There were other goldfinches, too, but this pair Pia always looked for. They seemed different from the other finches, livelier and more inquisitive. Once, the female had landed on Pia's foot and pecked at her straw sandals. Another time, it had landed on her arm, delicately selecting a crumb from Pia's sleeve.

Pia liked to watch the bird pecking for crumbs in the dirt and then lifting off, swooping and diving and warbling. Up into the sky, off into the air—where was she going? Pia often watched her fly off in the direction of the river, and then across it. Did she visit the castle, and if she did, why did she return here, to the dusty village, to nest?

16

Royal Duties

When the King, the Queen, Prince Gianni, and Princess Fabrizia entered the reception chamber, the Count and Countess rustled to attention. The Count bowed low. The Countess curtsied, her cheeks puffed as if she were barely holding in the words which wanted to spill forth. It was the custom, however, not to speak until the King had spoken.

The King was uncomfortable in his stiff linen shirt and golden brocade cape, and he could barely contain his displeasure. "Good evening," he managed.

As the Queen smiled at the plump pair

before her, the Countess lowered her gaze. *Those eyes!* thought the Countess. *So beautiful and so, so . . . unnerving.* But the Countess, barely able to contain her need to talk, was not disconcerted for long.

"We are so honored," she gushed.

The Count, unwilling to let his wife gain a head start on him, rushed in with, "*Deeply* honored and, if I may say—"

"Always a delight!" burbled the Countess. "A deeply honorable and—"

"—most humbled—"

The Queen knew they could go on like this for some time, and so she made her way to a chair beside the fireplace, sank into it, and said, "How nice to see you. How *very* nice to see you again."

Now the Count and Countess beamed at Prince Gianni.

"Prince Gianni, Heir to the Throne of Corona, it is our honor—"

"Our *deeply sincere and humble* honor—"

For Princess Fabrizia, the Count and Countess outdid themselves in flattery.

"How beautiful you are!"

"Like a fresh rose!"

"Your silken hair—"

"You must be the envy of all—"

The Princess accepted their compliments, but she was restless. For the second time that day, she wondered, *What is all this loveliness for?*

It was not until after the long dinner, after all the courses and all the toasting and all the polite conversation, that the one interesting bit of talk occurred. The Queen and the Countess were seated at a dressing table, powdering their faces, when the Countess asked about the hermit.

"How is your hermit?" she inquired.

"He is not *my* hermit," replied the Queen. "He is the King's hermit."

The Countess was wrestling with the horn-like protrusions on her wimple. "He must be—I suppose—*useful* to the King."

"I suppose he is. I've been contemplating acquiring my own hermit." The Queen was astounded that she had admitted this to the babbling Countess and immediately regretted it. She should have waited until she had actually acquired a hermit of her own.

The Countess was intrigued. "You *have?* How—how—perfect! How unusual! Do you have a hermit in mind?"

"No. I was thinking of a woman."

"A *woman?* A female hermit?"

"Yes," said the Queen. "I shall have a search begun—"

The Countess clapped her hands together. "But there is no need! I know of the perfect hermit! The absolutely most perfect hermit for you!"

17

The Wordsmith

After the royal family and their guests had refreshed themselves following dinner, they gathered for the evening's entertainment in the antechamber. It was a small square room embellished with gray marble walls and floors, burgundy taffeta drapery, and richly woven tapestries. The heavy wooden chairs were laden with cushions in vibrant colors: golds and purples and deep blues.

On this evening's schedule was the Wordsmith, who would recount a story. Neither the Count nor the Countess looked forward to the entertainment. It was hard for them to remain still and quiet, and it was especially hard to remain so when the Wordsmith told a story, because his mellow voice made them sleepy. The Count and Countess would have much preferred to continue conversing.

The royal family, however, was always relieved when it was time for entertainment, for it meant that they no longer had to bear the burden of talk. The Wordsmith took them away from their daily duties and mundane concerns. He took them to places they had not seen, to people they had not met—interesting, lively people—not the same dreary round of castle guests.

The King liked to hear tales of other kings, noble and brave. Prince Gianni, heir to the throne, preferred tales of melancholy young men who blossom into poets or artists. His younger brother, Prince Vito, sought stories of adventure: of dashing, energetic knights conquering dragons. Princess Fabrizia was most enchanted by stories of beautiful young princesses who save wounded princes.

The Queen enjoyed all of these tales, but

most of all she enjoyed the ones where a young woman—unnoticed and cast aside—becomes the heroine through her quick-wittedness and common sense. The Queen marveled at the Wordsmith's ability to spin words into scenes so vivid that she would forget that she was the Queen in the Castle Corona, so vivid that all the while he spoke, she was elsewhere, completely and entirely transported away.

The Wordsmith was a slender man, thirty years old—a bit younger than the Queen—with a modest air about him, at least when he entered the room. Once he began telling a story, however, he would become each character, noble or daring or meek or wicked, as the story demanded.

On this evening, he was clothed in his usual garb of black tunic and breeches beneath a swirling black velvet cloak. He carried a black velvet bag and smiled his gentle smile at each person in attendance. He was tall and limber, with wavy black hair, brown cow eyes, a slim face, and smooth, pale skin.

It was the Wordsmith's custom to ask the

King if he had a preference for a particular kind of story, and then turn to the Queen and to each of the royal children, and finally to the guests, to hear their preferences. He would then open his velvet bag and stare inside. No one ever saw the contents of this bag, nor did he ever remove anything from it, but he apparently gathered some sort of inspiration therein.

"King Guido, your preference for a tale this evening?" the Wordsmith asked.

The King thought a moment. "Let us have a king, a noble king, with a noble queen. The king saves the kingdom."

"And Queen Gabriella?"

"Perhaps a woman—not a queen—who helps to save the kingdom? And—and—perhaps, also a thief?"

"A *thief?"* said the Countess.

"A *thief*?" echoed the Count.

The King opened his mouth to object to his wife's suggestion because he did not want to be reminded of the castle thief, but when he saw the look on the Queen's face he reconsidered. A tale of a thief might help him determine how to handle the castle thief.

"Yes," the King said. "Let us have a thief."

"Yes, yes, a thief!" burbled the Countess, clapping her hands.

Prince Gianni said, "If we have a thief, then we must have a prince who quietly discovers the thief's identity."

"And a daring knight who kills him and saves the realm!" added Prince Vito.

Princess Fabrizia smoothed the lace at her cuffs. "And," she added impatiently, "a beautiful princess who—who—does something."

The Wordsmith opened his black velvet bag and stared inside.

Once upon a time, in a faraway land, lived a noble king. . . .

18

The Burden

While the Wordsmith was relating his story to the royal family and their guests, Pia and Enzio were on their way to Signora Ferrelli's. Their master was off visiting his mother (or so he said; Pia and Enzio suspected he was drinking ale with his friends), leaving orders for them as he departed.

"Clean up this place, you idle hogs, and don't let anyone come barging in," he had said. "There are thieves about, you know!"

"Thieves?" Pia had asked.

The master pounded the table with his fist. "Thieves! Guard my house!"

Pia viewed the dirt floor, the single tilting

chair, the scuffed and splintered table. *What*, she wondered, *would a thief want from here?*

As soon as their master left, Pia and Enzio slipped out and raced to the river's edge. The sun was round and golden, like a shining medallion nearing the horizon, darkening the surrounding hills to a deep purple. From their tree, they retrieved the leather pouch and made their way along the dusty alleys which led to Signora Ferrelli's dwelling. They had been troubled by Franco's warning that the King's Men would be swarming, searching for the thief, and they were anxious to deliver the things they had found, to be rid of their guilty burden.

"But what if we cannot trust the old woman Ferrelli?" Enzio asked. "What if she turns us in? What will be done to us?"

"We are only doing what we were told," Pia replied. "If we found an object, we were to give it to Signora Ferrelli. That's what the King's Man said."

"But can we trust *him?*" Enzio asked.

Pia had wondered this herself, and she was

not sure how to answer her brother. She glanced at the rough flour sack that Enzio carried. The pouch was hidden in it, beneath bunches of blue and purple grapes. "We see what the air feels like. You understand?"

"You mean, we don't give it to her unless—"

"Unless it feels right."

"And how will we know?"

"We'll know," Pia said. "We'll know."

Deep shadows cloaked the huts they passed, wrapping the simple dwellings in eerie layers of secrecy. Here and there candles burned within, casting sinuous shadows on the walls: an old man bending over a table; a cat stalking along a ledge; a long arm reaching upward. All was quiet, except for the occasional burst of a dog's barking or the low roll of voices from within the huts. As the air rapidly cooled and darkness fell, gray mist swirled amid the deepening shadows. Pia and Enzio had often been out in the night but they had never before felt the undercurrent of fear as they did now, carrying their hidden treasure.

Signora Ferrelli's cottage was along the lane, beyond a sharp curve to the left. Rounding this curve, they could make out the hazy outline of the Signora's tilting wooden cottage wrapped in low fog. A single lamp burned within. As they hesitated, the door opened and a large, dark figure emerged. So dense was the fog that the figure looked like a sooty phantom issuing forth into the night. Pia grasped Enzio's arm and pulled him back into the shadows.

This was not Signora Ferrelli, and they did not have to wait long to discover who it was, for they heard a familiar voice say, "I will then, I will." The door closed, and the dark figure turned down the lane in their direction.

"Our master!" Enzio whispered. "Pangini!"

"Quick!" Pia urged. "Run—as fast as you can—in case he goes straight home. He will be a tiger if he finds us gone. Tell him I've gone to—to—I don't know—think of an excuse. Hurry now, run!"

"But you—?"

"I'll see Signora Ferrelli. Run, run!"

Pia slipped between two narrow dwellings

as Enzio raced down the lane. Their master, head bowed low and mumbling to himself, shuffled past. At his slow pace, there was no danger that he would reach home before Enzio.

Pia tried to quiet her heart, beating rapidly like a trapped bird's. She didn't know why she was afraid. It was only the master, and she had endured his rages before. She felt as if the mist had invaded her mind, too, making things shift and change form. Why had the master been visiting Signora Ferrelli? His appearance there made her doubt their mission. Could they trust the old woman?

The pouch! Pia realized that, in the flurry, Enzio had run off still clutching the sack containing the leather pouch. That settled it, Pia thought. There was no reason to visit Signora Ferrelli now, and Pia might as well slip home. She made her way back out to the lane and glanced at the Signora's cottage. As she did so, the door opened, and the bent, slim figure of the old woman stood there, looking out. Pia moved toward her.

19

A Gift

Pia stood inside Signora Ferrelli's cottage. It looked much like Master Pangini's: dirt floors, straw mats, a single lantern burning. Here, though, were two cats. One, a calico, was nuzzling against Pia's leg. The other, larger one was midnight black and sat upright beside the hearth like a dark sentry, its green eyes glistening. A carved wooden cross hung above the rough-hewn mantel, but aside from the cross there was no adornment that Pia could see in the shifting light of the lantern. The air smelled of onions and potatoes and lavender.

Signora Ferrelli had not spoken as Pia came

to the door. The old woman had stepped aside, which Pia took as a sign for her to enter. The Signora was a small, thin woman, slightly stooped. Her hair was wiry and black, generously salted with gray. She was dressed all in black, as was the fashion for widows, and her clothes were of plain, rough cloth.

When the Signora finally spoke in her raspy voice, Pia flinched.

"So," the Signora said. "The night brings me another visitor."

"Oh?" Pia said, feigning ignorance. "You've had others?" She hoped the old woman would mention Master Pangini and suggest why he had been there, but Signora Ferrelli simply nodded. Pia wished she had told the truth, that she had seen the master leave. She might then have been able to ask, innocently, why he had been there.

The Signora seemed content to wait for Pia to divulge her purpose. The old woman stood silently, leaning on the single chair, a simple but finely crafted wooden one with a seat of woven rushes. Her look was steady and penetrating, somehow *knowing*, and it caused Pia a sharp pang of guilt. Pia wanted to be truthful, but was wary.

The calico cat purred against Pia's leg, prompting the Signora to say, "That cat is a good judge of character."

Pia reached down to stroke its fluffy back. "What is its name?"

"*Porco*. Pig. He eats a lot."

As Pia knelt and let the cat climb into her lap, the Signora eased herself onto the chair and placed her hands on her knees. "Porco does not like your master."

"Oh?" Pia said, avoiding the old woman's eyes. "Porco has met Master Pangini?"

"Porco hisses at him. That is the way with cats. They do not like someone, they hiss."

"Was Master Pangini your other visitor tonight—before me?"

The old woman's gaze suggested that she knew Pia's question was not so innocent. "Yes, Master Pangini was here. You smelled him?"

Pia's cheeks reddened. "Yes, I smelled him!"

"So, child, why have you come here tonight?"

"I'm not sure," Pia said. "I had questions, but—but now I am not so sure."

The old woman waited, still and silent like her black cat.

Pia's mind leaped here and there until she snagged a beginning. "You've heard about the thief?"

"Ah, the thief."

"We met a King's Man. He asked if we had found anything, something the thief might have dropped."

The Signora clicked her tongue.

Pia's hands fluttered in the air and then caught at her skirt, betraying her nervousness. "He said that if we found it, we should bring it to you." The old woman's silence was terrifying to Pia, and yet, at the same time, it was coaxing her to say more. "Why?"

Signora Ferrelli hoarsely echoed her: "'*Why?*'"

"Why *you*? Why did he say we should bring it to you—the object—*if* we found it?"

Signora Ferrelli shrugged. "People bring me things: secrets. I keep them."

"But if we found it, and if we brought it to you, would you keep that, too?"

The old woman stroked her cheek thoughtfully. "If it was mine to keep, yes. If not, no."

"But if it was not ours, and it was not yours, if it was what the thief dropped, and we brought it to you, what would you do with it?"

"Depends. Depends on many things, but I would know what to do when the time came. *If* the time came."

Pia did not feel she could or should say more. "You seem to—to know a lot."

"Ah," said the Signora, "an old chicken makes good broth. It's a saying, you understand?"

Pia did not understand, but she nodded anyway. Signora Ferrelli placed her bony hand on Pia's arm. "Wait," said the Signora. She crossed the room, disappearing briefly behind a rough cloth which shielded a straw pallet in the corner. When she reappeared, the Signora held a small packet wrapped in coarse linen. Handing the packet to Pia, she said, "For you and your brother. You might need them. Open later."

☙ 20 ❧

One Story Ends

Deep inside Castle Corona, all was silent in the chamber adjoining the dining hall, except for the Wordsmith's gentle voice, as he concluded his story:

. . . and so, as the thief lay dying, pierced by the sword of the young prince, the peasant girl knelt beside him. She mopped his brow and leaned close to hear his final words.

"'Twas only a sack of wheat," the thief whispered. "Was that so wrong?"

"No," said the peasant girl. "You were hungry."

And the noble king, recognizing the truth of the

peasant's words, declared that all should have bountiful wheat so that no one would be so hungry that he needed to steal.

The Wordsmith hesitated, taking in the attentive faces of the King and Queen, the royal children, and the Count and Countess, and then ended his story:

And they all lived happily thereafter.

Gentle applause followed. "Thank you, Wordsmith," the Queen said. "Another delightful tale."

"*Mm*, yes, thank you," echoed the King.

Disappointed, Princess Fabrizia pressed her hands to her cheeks. The princess in the tale was lovely, the most beautiful of all, but what had she done besides prance about wearing finery?

Prince Gianni was content, for the Wordsmith's story had included a melancholy poet. Prince Vito wondered about the energetic knight who had killed the thief. Was the

Wordsmith suggesting that the thief should *not* have been killed?

"Yes, yes," bubbled the Countess, "most enchanting—"

"And entertaining—" chimed the Count.

The Queen tapped her fingertips together. "But, I wonder what happens—next—to the peasant girl?"

The Princess waved her handkerchief. "What about the princess? What will she *do?*"

The Wordsmith stroked the velvet bag in his hands, as if calming its contents. "I will not know," he replied, "until I continue their story, another story."

"It is late," said the King.

This was the signal for the Wordsmith to depart and for the evening to end. The King and Queen bid their visitors a good night, and the servants escorted the Count and Countess and the royal children to their chambers.

The King was feeling twitchy. What he wanted to do was retire to his chamber and settle onto his feather mattress and drift off to sleep, but he first had to meet with the

Ministers of Inventory. He now regretted having ordered them to present their findings this evening.

The King was also rattled by the Wordsmith's story. Was no one else bothered that, in that tale, the thief had also tried to poison the king? *Poison the king*! Granted, the ruse had not worked because a young servant boy had tasted the soup first and died instantly, thus sparing the king. But still: *poison* the *king*? It was a most unpleasant thing to consider.

He had not enjoyed the ending of the Wordsmith's story, either. That peasant girl—did she really believe the thief did not deserve to be killed? Or to be punished in any way? And did the king in the story really give away wheat to everyone, for *free?* Who would pay for that wheat? The king?

The Queen, too, was out of sorts as she made her way to her chamber, but her thoughts were not about the Wordsmith's story. She had found it satisfying. What was on her mind now was the Countess's talk of knowing the perfect hermit for her. She was excited by the prospect of meeting this person, but she was also feeling unsure about her plan. She would have to prepare the King, to present the notion so that it sounded reasonable, possibly even arrange it so the idea seemed to come from the King himself. Yes, that would be the best course.

Prince Gianni, heir to the throne, lay on his bed staring at the ceiling. He thought he might compose a few lines of poetry, but he did not know how to begin. Which words to choose from the vast sea of words? He needed a velvet bag, like the Wordsmith's. What was in that bag? Words? Millions of words? Or a selection of the finest?

Princess Fabrizia stood before her Lady-in-Waiting. "Help me take off these—these—garments!" she said.

"The evening was not pleasant, Princess?"

The Princess tugged at her gown. "Oh, I don't know," she wailed. "I long to *do* something."

"Such as?"

"I don't know! *Something!* " And with that, the Princess collapsed onto her bed, sobbing.

Young Prince Vito leaped from the window ledge to a chest, slashing at the air with his sword. He thought of the Wordsmith's story, in which the young prince raced through the forest on his steed and captured the thief, throwing him to the ground and stabbing through his tunic. He *had* to stab the thief, didn't he? "Take that, thief! And that!"

The Wordsmith walked through the outer castle gardens, emptying his head of kings and queens and melancholy poets and peasant girls and thieves. He breathed in the cool night air, slowing his thoughts and his pulse. This was his usual post-story routine. He would make his way along the garden paths and down the slope to the hermit's dwelling, where, he knew, the hermit awaited him.

As the Wordsmith released himself from the evening's story, he felt a tremor in the ground, as if the enormous castle were subtly shifting, settling itself for the night. In the air, warm and cool currents realigned, suggesting to his fanciful mind intrigue and possibility.

21

The Cornos

Pia returned home from Signora Ferrelli's before Master Pangini. Enzio greeted her at the door, his cheeks flushed.

"Pia, so good you are here. I worried."

"The master—I saw him veer toward the alehouse. He'll be late coming in, and he'll be wobbling and stumbling and cursing," she said.

"I'm sorry I forgot to leave the pouch with you—"

"It's probably better," she said, scanning the room. "You hid it? Where?"

Enzio lifted his straw bedding. "See?"

"Good. I saw the Signora."

"Without the pouch?"

"Strange, Enzio, all strange. She didn't say why Pangini was there. She didn't say much of anything, but she gave me this." Pia withdrew the small packet from her pocket and offered it to Enzio.

He backed away. "No, you open it."

Pia carefully unwrapped the cloth and stared at its contents.

Enzio bent close. "The same—?"

"Nearly."

Inside the cloth were two small *cornos*, carved of red coral. Pia and Enzio rushed to compare them with the ones in the leather pouch which had been cast aside by the thief. The two new *cornos* were the same size as the others, the same shape, and appeared to have been carved from the same—or a very similar—piece of coral.

"I don't understand," Enzio said. "Where did she get them? Why did she give them to you?"

"She said they were for us, that we might need them."

"*Need* them? To ward off the evil eye?"

"Or danger, maybe, any kind of danger." Pia unraveled long threads from the linen cloth and slipped several through the loop at the end of each of the *cornos* that Signora Ferrelli had given her. "Here," she said, offering one to Enzio. "We will wear them—on long strings so we can hide them beneath our shirts."

Enzio fingered his *corno*, now dangling from his neck. "Looks like a chili pepper."

"Keep it hidden," Pia warned.

"And they will keep us safe?"

"We'll see."

22

The Inventories

The King was seated on his throne, pulling at his thick brocaded collar and scratching his neck. "Where *are* they?" he grumbled.

"Coming, Your Majesty," his Man-in-Waiting said.

"I hear them now."

The heavy oak doors opened and the black-and-red-cloaked Ministers of Inventory entered the room in single file. They looked nervous, some of them tugging at their sleeves, many with heads bowed low, a few mopping their brows.

"Spread out, spread out, so I can see you,"

the King ordered.

The ministers shuffled into place, bowing up and down like a row of bobbing blackbirds.

"Come, come, the report. What is missing?"

The ministers looked from one to another.

"Speak!" The sudden force of the King's thundered word slapped the ministers to full attention. The King's eyes roamed the line of faces, settling on one elderly man in the center of the line. "You there," he ordered, "speak!"

The minister bowed nervously. "Sire, we have completed our inventories to the best of our ability, given the short time—"

"I do not want excuses," said the King. It was hard for him to be stern. He did not like to do it, and it did not come naturally, but he was overtaken by a profound annoyance, roused by the news of a thief and by this disruption to the calm of his castle.

The minister who had spoken paled, the blood in his head plummeting to his feet. "Sire, it might be better if we reported our findings one by one."

The King's exasperation leaked out in a

long, heavy sigh. He swiveled to one end of the line. "You, then," he said, pointing at a minister. "Begin, and move down the line. Quickly, quickly!"

The minister cleared his throat. "Sire, I am the Minister of Inventory of Table Linens. We are missing one rectangular cloth, damask; and two napkins, linen; and one—"

"What?" boomed the King. "Who would want to steal a tablecloth and two napkins and—what else?"

"One tray cloth, silk—"

"Oh, bother! Is that it? That's what was stolen?"

The ministers shifted nervously, adjusting their robes. The next minister in line spoke rapidly. "Sire, I am the Minister of Inventory of Oats, and we are missing two sacks of oats."

"*Oats?*" boomed the King. "Two sacks of *oats*?"

The next minister also spoke rapidly, wanting to get it over with, hoping he would not add to the King's growing impatience. The minister knew he had to tell the truth, but he wished he could have lied. "Sire, I am the Minister of Inventory of the Queen's Jewels, and we are missing one pearl brooch."

The King slapped his knee. "There! There! That is more like it! A brooch, a pearl one, you say?"

"Yes, sire. Pearl with gold embellishment."

"Aha!" The King seemed oddly cheered.

The next minister said, "Sire, I am the Minister of Inventory of Silver, and we are missing one creamer lid, silver—"

"Ah! Silver. A creamer, you say? That would fetch a goodly sum."

"*Erm*, a creamer *lid*, to be precise," said the minister.

"Only the *lid?* Who would want a creamer *lid?*" The King's head was spinning. Missing oats, table linens, a pearl brooch, a creamer lid? He bid the remaining ministers report, and as they did so, he felt pummeled, a little here, a little there.

Each minister reported at least one thing missing. Among the missing objects were a pitchfork, twenty iron nails, two dinner plates, a looking glass, a bolt of silk cloth, a wooden stool, three knives, two wooden buckets, four tin ladles, a pair of boots, two velvet sashes, two kegs of ale, two chickens, three sheep, one cow, one rabbit, seven tallow candles, one iron candlestick, one linen tapestry, two chamber pots, three sacks of salt, eleven eggs, two pots of honey, four figs, one barrel of wine, eight bundles of hay, one crimson tunic, eight arrows, six horseshoes, one boar's head, one flute, and two cabbages. On and on they went, spewing forth the items missing from each of their inventories.

The King could not believe his ears. When they finished, he boomed, "A *boar's head*? A *cow*? *Cabbages*?" He wondered if he had entered one of the Wordsmith's stories. It sounded as if not one thief, but dozens, had invaded his castle. What was happening? Was this all but a bad dream from which he would awake?

The King dismissed the ministers with a wave of his hand and then he sat, still, on his throne. He would need to see the hermit. That was the only thing to do. But not now. He was so tired. In the morning he would visit the hermit and seek his wisdom.

23

Castle Dreams

"A *rabbit*?" said the Queen, when the King joined her and related the findings of the Ministers of Inventory. "*Figs?* A *cow*?" She conjured up the image of a thief making off with such things.

"It's not to laugh about," scolded the King.

"Sorry, Guidie, but—but—a *cow?* How do you think the thief made off with a cow without anyone noticing?" She placed her hand against her lips to cover the smile she could not contain.

It was easy enough for her to be amused, the King thought. *She* didn't have to solve the problem of the thief. She didn't have to sort out all these missing items and who had taken them and where they were now and how to find the thief (or thieves) and what to do with him (or them) once found.

Reading his mind, as she was often able to do, the Queen said, "Guidie, maybe the hermit can help."

"I've already thought of that."

She knew that, too, for the King always fled to the hermit whenever anything bewildered him. "Oh, Guidie," she said. "I'm feeling so—so—upset by all this." She leaned her head upon his shoulder. "I sometimes wish I had a hermit to go to, as you do. He must be such a comfort to you." She sighed heavily and raised her eyes to his.

He could not bear his queen to be upset, nor could he ever look into those violet eyes without shudders of tenderness. "*Shh*, Gabriella," he said, stroking her hair. "If having a hermit of your own would comfort you, then by all means, we will find you a hermit."

"Truly, Guidie? Truly? Oh, you are the most noble King, my dear beloved Guidie." This had been much easier than she had anticipated.

That night, the King tossed and turned, dreaming of thieves prowling the castle, snatching everything in sight: candles and chickens, tapestries and nails. He woke with his heart pounding when a thief had carried off his queen. The King nearly wept when he found the Queen sleeping peacefully in her chamber.

The Queen dreamed of a hermit: a woman cloaked in black, with long, flowing hair, who sat in a chair in her new hermitage and beckoned the Queen to join her, to speak of all that was in her heart.

Count Volumnia, who had drunk too much wine and eaten far too much, slept in a sound stupor. No dreams invaded his fuzzy head. The Countess, however, dreamed that she was crowned Queen and was mistress of the grand Castle Corona, and she was hurrying here and there seeking a seamstress who could make her coronation gown. *Gold, gold!* she said, to anyone who would listen. *It must be pure gold!*

Prince Gianni dreamed of walking through a meadow. Words fell upon him like soft raindrops, which he gathered and spun into poetry. The meadow ended abruptly at the river's edge, where he was lifted across by the breeze. On the far bank stood a peasant girl, who said, *Your words are jewels*. She did not know he was a prince, heir to the throne. She thought he was a poet.

Princess Fabrizia's dreams were of organdy and silk gowns flying out her window and sailing through the air. She had no clothes, except for a rough linen smock. From her window, she spied a young man on a golden horse. *Who am I?* she called to him. He turned away. He did not know.

Prince Vito, in his dreams, rode a white stallion out through the castle gates and thundered across the hills in pursuit of the thief. His sword, glimmering in the moonlight, slashed at the air. "You won't escape!" he shouted at the dark figure ahead of him. "Thief! Thief!" Prince Vito's words escaped from his dream and floated out his window and down into the courtyard, accosting the ears of the King's Men who stood guard.

"Thief? Someone's shouting *thief!*" Unaware that it was Prince Vito calling out in his dreams, the King's Men mobilized. They ran through the castle, swords drawn, checking each room. They mounted their horses and scoured the castle grounds and sped through the gates in search of the thief.

The King and Queen were awakened and alerted to the danger.

"Gather the children," the Queen said, grasping for her robe. "Bring them here. Oh, Guidie!"

The King, emerging from his own dreams of thieves, was dazed. Was this still part of the dream? He hated having to awake as the King, the one who had to make decisions. He searched for words.

"*Erm*. Find that thief!" he ordered. "Find him!" That would have to do, he decided. What else was there to say?

Count and Countess Volumnia huddled together in their chamber, quivering in terror. "We must leave this place," the Countess said, her chin trembling.

The Count agreed. "Yes, yes. First thing in the morning—"

"We'll make an excuse—"

"Mustn't sound too eager—"

"No, no, deepest regrets—"

"Profound disappointment—"

"Yes, that sort of thing," the Countess said, and they lay back against the pillows, wide awake and clutching each other, listening to the sounds of servants rushing up and down the halls.

24

The Intrusion

Master Pangini was awakened abruptly in the darkest hours of the night by fierce pounding at the door.

"What? *Oomf.* See to it, you dirty beetles!" The master was in a stupor. What idiot was making that racket?

Pia had been dreaming of Signora Ferrelli's two cats. They spoke to her. *Follow us*, they said, and so she was following them down a dark alley. Enzio was roused from dreams of chili peppers, deep red and hot on his tongue.

"Open up!" bellowed a voice beyond the door.

Enzio stumbled to the door, too groggy to be afraid. He thought someone might be in trouble, hurt or ailing.

A King's Man strode across the threshold, a fierce look on his face. His eyes scoured the room. With his sword, he pushed aside the rough cloth which draped the corner where Enzio and Pia slept. Pia clutched a shawl, covering herself. "What?" she asked. "What do you want?" She was seized with guilt, sure that the King's Man knew they had the leather pouch, but her guilt was coupled with anger at the man's boldness and his assumption that he could barge in anywhere he liked, frightening people at will.

Dashing to the opposite corner, the King's Man tore aside the master's curtain, catching him struggling to put on his trousers. The master raised his hands in surrender. "What do you want? What have we done?"

The King's Man scowled. "There's a thief on the loose."

"We have heard," the master said.

"No, another one. Tonight. You've seen no

one? You harbor no one?"

"No, no, no. No one here. It is only me and the dirty beetles."

Without further words, the King's Man left. Master Pangini wobbled to the center of the room, the ragged scar on his face paled to white, his barrel stomach straining at the shirt he had hastily donned. He snatched his leather strap from the table and slapped it hard on a stool. "Rubbish! Turnips! *Urg!*" He flailed for words to express his anger. "Barging in! Harboring—? Cabbage!"

25

Resolve

Rain pounded the dirt streets of the village, sending up puffs of dust and forming rivulets which snaked down the lanes and puddled in holes. Relentlessly, rain and wind swept over the rooftops, battering the small dwellings.

Dark clouds, heavy with more rain, hung low in the air.

Pia was up at dawn, although the dark clouds hid the early light which usually seeped in through the cracks around the door. She had been unable to sleep. The intrusion of the King's Man gnawed at her. "Enzio," she said, "Enzio, wake up. Listen. You listening?"

Enzio blinked, groggy and sluggish. "Almost awake," he said.

"Listen. We must see Signora Ferrelli today. We must get rid of the pouch. You agree?"

Her words jolted Enzio back to the night before. He was more than ready to be rid of that pouch. "Agree," he said.

Master Pangini, startled by a thunderous boom and the crack of lightning, awoke in a foul mood. Behind his curtain, he grumbled: "Idiots! Barging in!"

Pia rushed to light the fire. The master would be demanding and commanding, taking out his ire on her and on Enzio. She hastened to prepare porridge as Enzio stuffed rags under the door to stall the seeping rainwater.

They were surprised, though, when the master emerged. He was still grumbling, but not at them, and the look on his face was not one they were accustomed to. He sat heavily in his chair, stroking the scar on his face, deep in thought. Deep thinking was not his habit.

Pia and Enzio moved gingerly around the room, preparing the master's breakfast and exchanging puzzled looks. Would he suddenly erupt from this unusual state of quiet reflection? They were edgy, wanting to be prepared for whatever he might toss their way.

It was only after the master had eaten his porridge in silence that he spoke. "You stay here today. You keep watch. Understand?" He wasn't shouting. He didn't call them dirty beetles. "Understand?" he repeated.

It was easy enough to understand his instructions, but they did not understand this change in their master.

"I will be gone the full day. You must stay here and guard my house. I want your promise."

Enzio knew that Pia would promise easily, because she could make promises with no intention of keeping them if she thought the promises were silly, but Enzio did not want to make this promise. He wanted to go with Pia to see Signora Ferrelli and be rid of the pouch, and they couldn't do that if they had to stay here all day.

As Enzio suspected, Pia quickly said,

"Promise," and there was nothing he could do but echo her.

The master roused himself from his chair and headed out the door into cascading rain.

Pia stood in the center of the room, the lantern making her shadow tall and inky black on the wall behind her. "Don't know," she said. "Don't know what all that was about, do you?"

"*Puh!*" Enzio shook himself all over, as if shaking dust from his clothing. "It's a jumble, no? Why would he ask us to keep watch? Sounds dangerous."

Pia didn't answer. She busied herself with the normal motions of scraping the porridge pot so that she and Enzio could eat the remains, and with rescuing the stale end of a piece of bread and cutting it in two.

"And Pia," Enzio said, his mind still racing and eager to hear his sister's thoughts, "if we have to stay here, we can't go to the Signora's. We can't get rid of—"

"The pouch," Pia said. "I know."

A fierce boom shook the dwelling as rain pounded overhead. Drips seeped through the thatching, plunking onto the rush mats.

"Will we keep watch?" Enzio asked. "Will we stay here, or will we—"

Pia scanned the dark, wet patches over her head. "We will have to see what the day brings," she said. "You wearing your *corno*, Enzio?"

He pulled at the string around his neck, revealing the small piece of red coral hanging on it.

"Good," Pia said, releasing her own *corno* and stroking it gently. "Good."

26

Castle Conversations

"*Ewww!*" squealed Princess Fabrizia, covering her ears. "*Ewww!* I don't like thunder."

The Queen had joined the King in his chamber and had bid servants to set up cots for the royal children. She had not wanted them out of her sight while thieves were on the loose.

Prince Gianni lay on his cot, listening to the rain. He felt foolish, sleeping in his father's chamber. He, heir to the throne! But he was also comforted. He would not have liked being alone in his chamber with a thief prowling through the castle. He did not know how he could ever be King. If only he could be free to wander the meadows composing poetry.

Prince Vito slept soundly, oblivious to the disruption that his dreams and shouts had caused. His Man-in-Waiting had been unable to rouse him and had had to carry him to the King's chamber. Several times in the night Prince Vito called out again in his dreams: "You cannot flee!" and "I am the Prince!" These mutterings cheered the King and Queen amid their worries. "Isn't he darling?" the Queen said. "Heroic in his dreams."

Now, in the morning, as the rain continued to beat down on the castle walls, the King and Queen, Count and Countess gathered around the sturdy oak trestle table laid with fine white damask and porcelain plates emblazoned with the King's seal. The Count, sporting a purple tunic and purple hose, awaited the King's first words and then replied, "Your Majesty, such a night!"

The Countess, billowing in apricot organdy with matching wimple, burbled, "Your Majesty, such a ruckus—you must have been—not that it bothered us—"

"No, no," said the Count, "slept fine, like a dog, or a log, but we hope—"

"Oh, we do hope, all is well? Did you catch—"

"The thief?"

The King waved his hand dismissively. "The thief—much bother over trivialities. Come, sit, we eat."

Sudden thunder bellowed overhead, jolting the foursome. The Countess pressed her hands against her cheeks. "Oh my, oh my, oh my."

The King summoned the servants, who arrived carrying silver platters laden with pheasant eggs, steaming buns, dainty pots of porridge, cream, strawberries, pears, and slices of roast pork garnished with sprigs of rosemary. As the King lifted a warm roll to his lips, the Count said, "Sire, wait! I—pardon my—what I mean to say—"

The King was irritated. Could he not even eat his roll in peace?

"Sire, given the—sorry to mention it—the

thief, and the—how should I say—*strain?*—of last night, do you—?"

The Queen could not bear it. Normally, she would have kept silent and allowed the Count to babble on unintelligibly, but this morning she had no patience for it. "*What?*" she said. "What *are* you trying to say, Count?"

The Countess's lips pinched, as if she'd swallowed a sour grape; she was stung by the Queen's tone, aimed at her husband.

The Count rushed to complete his thoughts. "I was trying to suggest—have you, or do you, or, let me be blunt—"

"*Please do* be blunt," said the Queen.

The Count rushed on. "Well, then, my question is: Do you have a taster?"

The King and Queen exchanged glances. "A *what?*" the King said.

The Countess beamed. This was a magnificent question her husband was asking.

"A taster," said the Count. "Someone to taste your food before you eat it." He said these last words slowly, the way he might speak to a child.

"A *taster*?" said the Queen, struggling to disguise her scorn.

"A *taster*?" echoed the King. "Why would I want someone to taste my food?" He snorted and bit into his roll.

The Count, ruffled, did not touch his food. "You've heard about Count Malpezzi, I assume?"

The Countess leaped in. "Oh, Count Malpezzi, terrible, terrible."

"Terrible, terrible *what?*" asked the Queen, who had replaced her roll on her plate without taking a bite.

"*Poisoned!*" boomed the Count triumphantly.

Thunder rumbled overhead, rattling the dishes. The Countess clutched the edge of the table. "Yes, yes, poisoned, in his food, in his soup—"

"Died instantly."

"Instantly!"

The King stopped chewing, his roll dry in his mouth.

"Poisoned?" said the Queen. "By whom?"

"Don't know," said the Count, satisfied that his hosts were now interested in what he had to say.

The Countess tapped her cheeks. "A servant? An intruder? No one knows!"

The Count, who had still not touched his food, said, "It might be wise, therefore, given the thief—"

"And the ruckus, the disturbing—"

"It might be wise to engage a taster, that's all I am—most humbly—suggesting, Your Majesty."

The King, with some difficulty, swallowed the remains of his first bite of warm roll, the kind of roll he had previously so enjoyed.

27

Cottage Conversations

An odd hush had descended over the village. The rain had slowed to a drizzle of fine mist, but heavy clouds, like bundles of soiled laundry, hung low in the sky. There were none of the usual shouts of the villagers or the creaking and rattling of carts in the lane. Pia and Enzio had spent the morning cleaning and cooking and mopping up the water, swirling with dust and clay, that had invaded the cottage.

"Curious, this quiet," Pia said.

Enzio peered out the door. "Don't like it."

Shortly before bells chimed the noon hour, Master Pangini returned. Pia had his meal ready, but he did not stay long enough to eat it. "You are here?" he said. "You haven't left?"

"No," Enzio said. "We haven't left."

"Remember your promise. You stay here today, all day." He ducked back out the door and hurried down the lane.

"I could sneak to the market," Pia said. "See what Franco is saying—"

"No. We *promised*."

"I don't want to be stuck here all day!" Pia snatched at the master's dirty clothes lying on the floor. "Here, then, you'll have to help me. Lug these to the rain barrel out back."

Enzio scowled at the mound of laundry. *If I were a prince,* he thought, *I would not throw my clothes on the floor, but someone else would wash them for me, and they would be fine clothes, and I would have a fine horse, a white one.*

Pia, whose mind often traveled the same lanes as her brother's, said, "Enzio, if I were a princess, I would never have to soil my hands again, ever! And no one would tell me what to do or call me a dirty beetle. I could do whatever I chose—anything, anything at all."

"And we would eat pheasant and sweet cakes—"

"And I would wear silken gowns—"

"—upon a white horse—"

"—and we wouldn't have a care in the world!"

28

Greener Grass

Against her better judgment, the Queen led the Countess to her favored spot, the secluded hornbeam tunnel. Normally, as soon as she entered its shelter, the Queen felt calm. Deep green leaves swirled overhead, blocking out all but the most slender shafts of light, and the long path ahead of her looked safe and comforting and smelled so fresh, with the distinct, slightly tangy aroma of the leaves and bark.

The Queen always walked here alone. It was her sanctuary. On this day, however, she included the Countess, for she needed a private place to speak. She regretted her decision the moment they entered the tunnel, when the Countess began chattering.

"Oh, how divine, how exquisite!" The Countess clapped her hands. "Isn't this—isn't this—so quaint and—"

It was dry on the path, so densely interlaced were the branches overhead, but the Queen could smell the rain that had washed the outer roof of leaves. She searched for words with which to stop the Countess's chatter. She decided to be blunt, to get to the point immediately, and so she asked about the hermit.

"She is the most perfect hermit for you," the Countess replied. "She came instantly to mind."

Despite the Countess's rushing words disturbing the normal calm of the hornbeam tunnel, the Queen was enchanted. Soon she would have her own personal hermit. When they came to the end of the tunnel, the Queen felt a surge of joy, for there, off to the right, stood a timber storehouse, and the Queen recognized that it would make a perfect cottage for her hermit.

"I'll have the servants clean it, of course," she said to the Countess, "and add some beautiful tapestries—"

"Oh, no," scolded the Countess. "You must not do *that*."

The Queen, not used to having anyone tell her what she must or must not do, looked sharply at the Countess.

"Forgive me, Your Majesty, forgive me. I am only suggesting—I believe that a hermit is supposed to live *sparely*. They *like* it that way, hermits. I think you might also want to suggest she let her hair grow long and wild, and let her fingernails grow, and—"

The Queen tried to compose herself. The Countess might go on like this for hours. "Countess, how long are you planning to stay?"

"I am so sorry to say—it is with deep regret—such a disappointment I cannot tell you—but we must depart—the Count has urgent matters—"

"Ah, yes, so disappointing." The heavens echoed the Queen's inner joy at the impending departure of her chattering guests: the sun burst briefly through the clouds, its rays making the grass sparkle like a carpet of tiny diamonds.

The King nearly skipped through the gardens as soon as the carriage carrying the Count and Countess departed. The paths were wet and the benches damp, but still the King chose to admire the puddles and to settle himself on a bench so that he could sort his thoughts.

He tried to rid his mind of the Count's talk of poison. The Count had gone on for some time about the necessity of a taster. *A taster!* It had sounded utterly ridiculous at first, but as the Count prattled on, the King began to worry. After breakfast, during which everyone's appetite was diminished, the King, in part to attempt to silence the Count, had said, "Fine, fine. I'll see to it. One of the servants can be my taster."

"I am not sure that is best," the Count said. "I would not presume to have your wisdom in this matter, but how could you be sure that the servant was not a poisoner? *Mm?*"

It was all the King could do to disguise his

astonishment. One of his servants? A *poisoner*? Never!

"It was thought—suspected—that it was one of Count Malpezzi's own servants who poisoned him. Never proven, but suspected. I think they hanged the servant anyway, yes, I think they did. You might want to choose someone outside the castle, *mm?*"

Now the King sat on the damp bench, trying to dismiss the Count's warnings. There was so much to say to the hermit. There was the new thief, of course, and this taster business, and the inventories—oh, so much to tell the hermit. At the edge of the path, a pile of leaves, blown from their branches in the morning's storm, rustled. They shifted and rose and then fell again, revealing the black, wet body of a snake.

"You! Again!" the King cried, leaping up from the bench and rushing down the path, hurtling headlong toward the hermitage.

29

Free?

In the village, in Master Pangini's hut, the day stretched on so long that it seemed to Pia that the sun and earth were stalled, and that the morning's storm had captured the air around them and fled with it to some distant land.

"Why did Pangini say to 'keep watch,' Pia? Keep watch on *what*?"

"Or for what, Enzio." She touched the *corno* hidden beneath her smock, for reassurance. "I don't think I can scrub another wretched pot or wash another dirty shirt or beat another moldy mat. I feel like a prisoner."

"In a dungeon," Enzio added.

They were grateful when the long-awaited darkness finally slipped over the village, so they could curl up on their straw mats and sleep and hope that tomorrow they would be free to leave, to scour the village for news and, more urgently, to be rid of the pouch and the guilt it brought them.

Dawn, too, came slowly, limping, as if the burden of shedding the night required strenuous effort. An odd, reddish-orange glow bled low across the sky as Pia pried open the door to peer out.

They had heard the master come in late, not stumbling or shouting as he so often did, but shuffling purposefully across the room to his bed. When he awoke, he seemed not to know how to behave. He tried on a few grumbles, but they were awkward grumbles, not his usual boisterous, forceful tirades. "Porridge is too lumpy. Well, it is. Dirty—radish—*mmf*." He thumped the table when he wanted something, so that they had to scurry to interpret his demands.

"No, not more porridge. More—that—"

Behind his back, Pia and Enzio opened their mouths in mute, frustrated screams.

As the master was departing, without yet having given any orders for the day, Enzio said, "Master? Can we leave today?"

"Leave?"

"I need to go to the market," Pia said.

"And am I to relieve Rocco today?" Enzio added.

Pangini roused himself, his voice booming in its old, familiar way. "Of course, you idle turnips! You think you're going to lie around here all day? Clean this place up and then get to the market and—and, do all those things you're supposed to do! *Hrmph!* " And with that, he slammed the door behind him.

"Free!" whispered Enzio.

Pia tapped her *corno*, once, twice. "Free!"

Some of the usual noise had returned to the village. Carts rumbled through the streets and villagers shouted to one another, but fewer people were about, and those who were out were jumpy and cautious.

"Something strange going on, Enzio."

"And Franco will know what."

They were disappointed, however, when they reached the market and found no sign of Franco. They asked about him at several stalls, but the responses were not what they expected. Most people looked around before they responded, their answers silent gestures: a shrug, a shaking of the head, a roll of the eyes, all suggesting "Who knows?" or "Who cares?"

Pia helped Enzio during his shift at the stall, busying herself piling up oranges and grapes and melons, stacking them in attractive groupings. Few people spoke except to ask for this or that fruit or vegetable.

"All strange, Enzio, very strange, don't you think?"

"No one's talking."

Around her waist Pia had tied the narrow, coarse sack which contained, deep inside, the leather pouch, and from time to time she could not help but reach for it, to reassure herself that it was there. In the tense quiet of the marketplace, she feared that someone might snatch the sack from her, or kidnap her, holding a sword to her neck.

When Rocco reappeared, Enzio and Pia raced down the dusty lanes, bound for Signora Ferrelli's. The red of the early dawn had long disappeared and now dirty gray clouds gathered overhead, pushed by wind that carried with it an eerie but soothing lavender aroma, as if, Pia imagined, the wind had first swept through grand castle gardens.

When they reached the Signora's dwelling, they tapped at the door and waited. They tapped again. They knocked louder.

"Maybe she can't hear," Enzio said.

"She heard well enough the other night."

They slipped around the side of the hut, stopping at a narrow window at the back. Pia slowly parted the oilcloth draped over the window. It was dark inside. No fire was lit. No sign of the Signora.

"She's gone out, probably," Enzio suggested. "To the market."

Pia thought they would have passed her on the way. The room appeared odd, but she didn't know why. And then, she felt a peculiar throbbing from the *corno* around her neck.

"Enzio, come with me," she said, hurrying back to the door.

"You're not going *in*?"

Pia's answer was evident. She had already pushed against the wooden door and stepped over the threshold. She stood there a moment and then backed out.

"Enzio, she's gone."

"I knew *that*."

"No, I mean completely gone. She had a big cross on the wall. It's gone, and her cats are gone, too."

Enzio and Pia returned to the marketplace. They walked the cramped aisles, hoping to catch someone gossiping.

"Pia, he's back." Enzio pulled at Pia's arm, leading her to the far end of the marketplace. There, on his stool, sat Franco, and around him gathered a small pool of villagers. Pia and Enzio had to slip in close because Franco was speaking in softer tones than usual.

". . . and I tell you, they came even to my home," Franco was saying.

"And mine," a villager said.

"Mine, too."

"Everywhere!"

"Shouting and swords drawn—"

"Looking for a thief!"

"Another one?"

Franco bit off a piece of bread and spoke with his mouth full. "*Mmf.* More thieves."

"But not from *here*?" said one thin, wrinkled woman.

"Where *else* then, if not here?" Franco said.

Audible gasps swept through the small gathering, passed from one to another around the circle.

"You've heard about the old woman Ferrelli?" Franco said.

"No, what?"

"They've taken her."

"*Who* has taken her?"

Franco munched at his bread. "Them, of course. The King's Men."

"No!"

"Not the Signora!"

"But why?"

Franco leaned forward, conspiratorially. "I hear she might be one of the thieves."

"No!"

"Never!"

"Impossible!"

Franco chomped into his bread. "I do not know if it is true. It is what I hear, that's all I can say."

"But where has she been taken?"

Franco chewed his bread slowly, swallowed, and leaned even farther forward, so that his great bulk was precariously perched on the small stool. "Where else?" he said. "To the dungeon. The castle dungeon."

"No!"

"Never!"

"Is there a *dungeon* at the castle?"

Franco shrugged. "Isn't there a dungeon at *every* castle?"

Pia and Enzio left the market and slowly made their way home.

"The Signora?" Enzio said. "You think she's a thief?"

"No. Can't be so. But then—"

"What?"

Pia stopped to tap her foot in a puddle. The water soaked through her straw sandal as she stared at the water. "She is mysterious, you agree?"

Enzio leaned down to retrieve a round pebble from the puddle. "Spooky, too."

"But why would she give us these?" Pia tapped at the *corno* beneath her smock.

Enzio examined the pebble, black from the water, with a single sparkling fleck embedded in one side. "Maybe she *stole* them. Maybe she had to get rid of them."

Pia reached for the sack at her side. "Then—*ack*—then we have more stolen things. I don't like it."

Nearing Pangini's cottage, they heard deep voices. Outside stood two King's Men, talking to an old man. Spotting Pia and Enzio, the old man shook his head vigorously and said loudly, "No, I don't know where Pangini is, or the children."

"No need to shout, old man."

"I am sorry, I do not hear so good, and so I talk loud."

Pia and Enzio backed away, and they might have escaped entirely had they not retreated directly into the path of two more King's Men.

30

Kidnapped

The King's Men swooped up Pia and Enzio in the lane outside Master Pangini's hut and placed them high up on horses, a King's Man grasping each child as they raced through the village. Pia trembled as she caught the look on Enzio's face: pure terror. She was not able to comfort him, either in look or word, so terrified was she, too. She was certain they were being taken to the dungeon, certain they would be accused of being the thieves—and why not? At her waist was the sack which held the leather pouch.

On that terrifying ride through the village and over the bridge across the winding Winono

River and up the hillside toward the towering castle, she was certain, too, that it was Signora Ferrelli who had betrayed them. Pia wished she had not sought her out, wished she had never heard of the terrible woman. Her heart beat wildly, as if it were straining to escape and fly off into the sky. She wished she could release the sack, drop it, but how could she do so without the King's Men noticing? They were doomed. Doomed.

On they rode, the horses' hooves pounding loudly, the smell of their sweat rising from their straining bodies, and the grasp of a King's Man tightly wound around each child, not, Pia knew, for protection, but so the King's Men would keep their bounty—the thieves!—firmly in their grasp. They passed through the mist hovering over the river and burst into sunlit meadows and saw—the closest Pia and Enzio had ever been to it—the enormous Castle Corona looming ahead, coming closer and closer, and they were sure they were riding to their deaths.

When the King's Men surged through the

gate in the wall that encircled the castle and its grounds, Pia felt she was shrinking, so vast were the walls through which they entered, so grand was the hillside enclosed by the walls, so tall was the castle. She could barely breathe.

The King's Men halted beside a stone building, from which an old, bent man emerged. "These the ones?" asked a King's Man. The old man nodded, and the King's Men rode on, skirting lush gardens bustling with servants and guards. A chicken flapping noisily was snatched up by the neck and flung over the shoulder of a man carrying a hatchet. Catching Enzio's eye, Pia rubbed her throat and smiled weakly, in a vain attempt to reassure him.

The King's Men dismounted, pulling Enzio and Pia roughly from the horses, and led them through a tall entryway, a vast stone arch, beyond which was another courtyard. Enzio and Pia gaped. It looked like a luxurious miniature village, with swept paths and a vast circle of buildings all joined together by the castle walls rising high overhead. Servants darted here and there, in and out of dark entries. Midway up one side, gold-and-red flags flew above balconies draped with trailing flowers.

"To the King!" a King's Man shouted as he dragged Pia past servants who had stopped to observe the two scruffy children being pulled along. Pia strained to look back at Enzio. He looked so frightened. She pulled her arm loose from the King's Man and rushed to her brother, hugging him tightly, clinging to him.

"Come on, come on, move along!"

They were shoved and dragged through a long, dark hall and up stone steps to a dark, massive wooden door studded with iron. One of the King's Men disappeared inside, then returned several minutes later for Enzio and Pia.

"Go on, then, stand at the back."

They were pushed through the door and into a vast chamber with gleaming marble floors and tall, narrow windows draped with masses of rich cloth, and there, at the far end, on a raised platform were two thrones, and on them sat the King and Queen.

Enzio thought he might be sick, right there

on the marble floor, so shocked was he to be in the presence of the King and Queen. Pia's spirits, however, lifted. "*The King!*" she whispered. "*The Queen!*"

"Stand here," ordered a King's Man, as he marched up to the thrones. Pia and Enzio could hear the buzz of his words but could not make out what he said. They saw the King's Man step aside as the King and Queen observed them. The King mumbled something, and the King's Man returned to where the children were standing.

"Follow me," he ordered, leading them out of the chamber.

Pia's anger flared. "He should at least have spoken with us!"

One of the King's Men chuckled. "Spoken? With *you?*"

"Yes," she said. "With us. He shouldn't send us to the dungeon without a word!"

"Ha! The dungeon! Ha, ha, ha!" The other King's Men joined him in his hearty laughter. "Ha, ha, ha!"

"What amuses you so?" Pia demanded.

The King's Man held her arm tightly. "And who are you, child, to be talking so freely with the King's Men?"

"I am Pia, and I want to go home."

"Oh, I know your name, child." To the other men, he said, "Did you hear that? She wants to go home, to that hovel with the gruff Pangini!"

The men all laughed. "Ho!" one of the men said. "Ho, that's good, that one. Home to the hovel of the gruff Pangini!"

"Don't scoff at my sister," Enzio exploded. "We do want to go home."

"Ha, ha, ha. Ha, ha, ha." The men laughed on and on as they ushered the children down the stone steps and across the courtyard.

Just before entering a darkened doorway, Enzio called to Pia. "There!"

Pia followed his glance. Crossing the courtyard was Signora Ferrelli with her two cats.

In a

Towering Castle . . .

31

The New Hermit

Some people relish change, welcoming the excitement it brings to otherwise predictable days. Others, however, are unsettled by change, unable to relinquish safe and familiar habits. Prince Gianni, heir to the throne, was one of the former, delighted that there were new people about, beyond the usual string of visiting diplomats and tiresome tutors.

His mother's new hermit was residing in the castle for a few days while her dwelling, the storehouse at the end of the hornbeam tunnel, was being readied. What a curious woman: lean and wrinkled, with eyes that seemed to take in everything at once—from a person's clothing and stature and even, somehow, his thoughts, to the light, the marble floors, the rich tapestries.

The new hermit was followed everywhere by her two cats, a plump calico and a mysterious black one. The black one crept along in a stately way, a king among cats.

On one of these mornings when the new hermit was residing in the castle, the Prince saw her in the hall as he left the breakfast chamber. The calico cat was winding in and out between the old woman's ankles, mewing. The black one sat beside her. The hermit had stopped one of the servants, who was carrying a silver tray laden with leftover food.

"What's this?" the hermit said. "Pheasant eggs? Pork? Where will it go now?"

"*Shh*," the servant girl said, "the Prince will hear you."

"So? So he hears me." The old woman took a slice of pork from the tray and popped it into her mouth. "Mmm, tasty."

The servant girl flushed. "Prince Gianni, heir to the throne, I am so sorry, I didn't—I couldn't—"

Prince Gianni smiled benevolently. "Let her have as much food as she likes." He expected the hermit to thank him profusely, but she did not. She reached for a pheasant egg and tucked it into her mouth. "Mmm!"

The Prince longed to offer a poetic image, to impress the hermit. "A pheasant egg is like a—a—" His mind wobbled, searching for the right word. *A stone? A cloud? A pear?*

The hermit swallowed and finished the Prince's sentence, bluntly. "It's like a chicken egg."

Prince Vito emerged from the breakfast chamber as the hermit reached for another egg. "You there!" he bellowed. "Stop that!"

The hermit did not stop. The black cat at her side put one paw forward, preparing to pounce.

The servant girl quivered, rattling the dishes on the tray. "I am so sorry, Prince Vito, I—"

"Stop! Do you hear me?"

"Vito," his brother said, "I have given the hermit permission to eat."

"Why did you do *that*?"

Prince Gianni straightened his back, unconsciously adopting a kingly stance.

"Because," he replied, "I wanted to."

"Permission?" the hermit said. "I have never before expected permission to eat."

Prince Vito glared. "You are in the Castle Corona now, and you must—"

Prince Gianni put a hand on his brother's shoulder, restraining him. "I will take care of this, Vito."

As Prince Vito stomped off, Princess Fabrizia emerged, followed by her Lady-in-Waiting, who was brushing crumbs from the Princess's gown. Regarding the hermit's tattered black dress, the Princess said to her brother, "Is that what she is going to *wear*?" She spoke as if the hermit were invisible. "And is she not going to comb her hair?"

The old woman swallowed the remains of a sweet roll and said, "These are my clothes. They have served me fine these many years. And this'—she reached up to pat her hair—'I am glad I have hair on my head to keep it warm, and whether it be smooth or tangled is no matter to me." She plucked the last remaining pheasant egg from the tray and slipped it into the mouth of the calico cat.

The King emerged next. He was not one who enjoyed change. It irritated him. He was glad that the Queen now had her own hermit and was so happy as a result, but he wished the old hermit woman would be out of his sight, for she flustered him. She was so unlike his own silent, calm hermit. This woman, this hermit, was a prickly presence, speaking whenever and whatever she liked.

The King regarded his son and daughter, the servant girl, and the hermit. Preferring to avoid the hermit altogether, he mumbled, "Have to—matters to attend—*hrmph*—" and, giving the group a wide berth, he strode down the hall in a kingly and preoccupied manner.

The Queen, last to leave the breakfast chamber, was thrilled to see her hermit. "Oh, hermit!" she gushed, rushing to the old woman's side. "Today your lodgings will be ready. I am so eager to show you!" She waved her hand at her children and the servant girl, dismissing them, and, taking the hermit's elbow, led her away.

32

The Tasters

Even more intriguing to Prince Gianni than the new hermit were the tasters, who had been brought to the castle shortly after the Queen's hermit had arrived. Prince Gianni did not understand the need for tasters, but then he had not been particularly attentive when his father, the King, had mumbled an explanation for their presence. All Prince Gianni knew was that the sole duty of these tasters was to taste the food of the royal family before they ate it. It sounded absurd to the Prince, but he was not one to dwell on such things.

During the King's last visit to his hermit, the hermit had listened silently to the King's explanation of the inventory results and the new thief-in-the-night and the Count's tale of the poisoned Malpezzi and the suggestion for a taster. To the account of the inventory results, the hermit had replied, after considering the information, "When one has nothing, nothing disappears."

"*Mm*, wise," the King had said. He did not know how this affected his own dilemma, with the missing cow and cabbages and whatnot, but it comforted him nonetheless.

To the account of the new thief in the night, the hermit said, "The mouse may say to the nut, 'In time, I will open you.'"

"Oh," said the King. "Oh. Mm." He tried to envision a mouse talking to a nut. He wondered what the hermit's words meant. *In time I will open you*. The King nodded sagely, disguising his bewilderment. These were surely wise words, he thought, so wise that he would need some time to understand them.

To the King's account of the tale of the

poisoned Malpezzi and the need for a taster, the hermit said, "He who sleeps catches no fish."

"Why, yes, yes, *mm*." The King could not fathom what these words meant. *He who sleeps catches no fish?* Well, of course, if one is sleeping one can't be catching fish, but what on earth did the hermit *mean?* Did he mean the King shouldn't *sleep?* Did he mean the King should *go fishing?* It was extremely perplexing.

As the King sat there trying to make sense of the hermit's words, he spied a black lump on the window ledge. Fearing it might be a snake, the King pointed to the object. "That—that—what is that?"

"Someone must have dropped it. I found it outside."

"It's not—it's not—a *snake*, then?"

"No, it is not a snake."

"It looks like—on closer inspection—" The King stood and approached the object with some caution. "Why, it is the Wordsmith's bag, is it not?" He touched the velvet bag, and although he wanted to lift it and even peer inside, he thought he shouldn't, that this would not be kingly.

The hermit remained seated on the floor. "Is it?"

"Yes, I think it is," replied the King. He was not sure what to do. Should he sit again, in case the hermit had more wisdom to offer? Should he offer to return the pouch to the Wordsmith? The King was reluctant to leave the calm hermitage. *Wait*, he thought. *I am the King. I can do whatever I please! And I am no errand boy. Let someone else return that pouch*. And so he sat. "You will sort that out, the Wordsmith's bag, getting it back to him?"

The hermit nodded.

"And the taster? What was that you said? About the fish?"

"He who sleeps catches no fish."

"Oh. Yes. Enormously wise. But do you think—would it be wise—should I acquire a taster?"

The hermit put his hands together, as if he were praying, lifted his hands to his lips, and closed his eyes. He sat in silence like that for several minutes, while the King tried his best to remain still. At last the hermit said, "Two."

The King was not sure he had heard correctly. "*Two* or *too* or *to?*"

"Two."

The King felt a throbbing in his head, behind his left eye. "To—too—two—?"

"Two tasters."

"Oh. I see. *Two*. Two tasters?" The King, at first relieved that he at last understood the hermit, was then stumped. "But why two?"

"Two are better than one," the hermit replied.

"Ah, of course."

The hermit placed his hands calmly on his knees. "Sire, would you like me to make the arrangements?"

"Yes! Why, that would be—yes, by all means."

The King left the hermitage feeling he was free of burdens. Of course, he would have to contemplate the hermit's words about the mouse and the nut and the sleeping person who catches no fish and all that, but at least the taster problem was resolved. It was only when the King was back in the castle that he wondered, but only briefly, *how* the hermit would make these arrangements. As far as the King knew, he was the only one the hermit ever spoke with. The King did not like the idea that his hermit would be speaking with someone else. Who would that be?

These thoughts evaporated when he reached his chamber and saw the empty bed which awaited him. A nap! He needed a nap.

33

Duty Calls

When Pia and Enzio first met the Mistress of Food in the hot and dimly lit kitchen, they were understandably confused. They had been abruptly kidnapped from their village and hurried to the castle, fearing for their lives all the while, roughly shoved here and there, and, just before meeting the Mistress of Food, they had seen Signora Ferrelli crossing the castle courtyard. The Signora was not in a dungeon; she was not in chains. In fact, she seemed to be wandering freely.

Enzio nudged his sister. "A spy, Pia. She must be a spy."

They had no time to dwell on Signora Ferrelli, because standing before them was a tall woman dressed in a long red smock covered with a crisp white apron. She had long, curly red hair pulled back with a plain black ribbon, and a pleasing, heart-shaped face. To Enzio and Pia's astonishment, the woman knelt before them and took their hands gently in hers.

"I am the Mistress of Food," she said, "but you may call me Giovanna. And you are—?"

"Enzio."

"Pia."

"Enzio," the woman repeated. "Pia." She viewed the children through blue eyes, blue as a bluebird, blue as the bluest flower in the meadow. "So you are the tasters."

"Tasters?" Pia said. "What's that?"

Giovanna glanced up at the King's Men and then back at the children. "So, they did not bother to tell you why you are here?" Giovanna studied the King's Men a moment and then dismissed them. "I will take charge now. Go on, go on—" She pushed at the air with her hand, much as she might shoo away chickens. Then she took Pia and Enzio by the hand and led them to a table in the corner, where she explained that they would be tasters for the King. "You will taste his food before he eats it."

"Taste his *food?*" Enzio said. He grinned, thinking it was the silliest thing he had ever heard.

"Why would we do *that?*" Pia asked.

Giovanna leaned closer and whispered. "The King has got it in his head that he might be poisoned."

Pia gaped. "*Poisoned?*"

"In his *food*?" said Enzio.

"I know it sounds silly, but kings get silly ideas sometimes."

"So, you don't really think someone would poison his food?" Pia asked.

Giovanna swatted the air. "*Pah!* Look around you. See all these women and girls? See how hard they are working? How gentle they are? You think they are going to poison anyone?"

Pia and Enzio studied the women standing before pots, stirring, and the young girls chopping, all of them laughing easily and chatting amiably as they worked. All wore simple red smocks and white aprons, and each had a plain ribbon or a small flower in her hair.

"So," Pia said, "you do not think we would be poisoned, then?"

Giovanna chuckled. "No, I do not think so, and you will have some good food to taste."

Enzio's eyes widened. "Like what?"

"Oh, cakes and sweets, roasted chicken and pheasant and pork, strawberries and—"

"Oh!" Pia said. "Oh!"

"Although, I do not know everything," Giovanna said, "and I have wondered—it has crossed my mind—that it *could* be possible that there is someone out there who would *like* to poison the King."

Enzio's spirit crumpled. "I would not like to be poisoned."

"We could *die*," Pia said.

Giovanna tapped her hands on her knees. "Now, now, let us not fret. You have been chosen to be the King's tasters, and you have no choice in the matter. If it will make you feel better, I will personally taste all the food before *you* do. That way, if it is poisoned, I would die, and you would not."

Pia breathed in the smell of roasting chicken. Enzio watched a cook drizzle warm chocolate over a pile of strawberries.

"Fine," Pia said. "We will do our duty."

"Yes," agreed Enzio. "When do we start?"

On the first day of their new position, they were given rooms in the dark, low-ceilinged servants' quarters and tasted the food in the kitchen where it was prepared. But on the second day, the King had said he wanted to see them taste his food, and he did not like having to summon them from below and wait for them to arrive. He had the servants move Pia and Enzio to a chamber nearer his own. Pia and Enzio's new room was larger than the whole of Master Pangini's hut. The ceilings rose high over them. Tall narrow slits in the walls, which served as windows, let in bright light in the early morning.

"Look, Pia, *beds*, not straw on the floor."

Enzio chose one of the two beds and sank onto it. "Try yours, Pia. They must be full of feathers, so soft!"

Pia stretched out on the other bed, noting the aroma of fresh linens, smoothing her cheek against the soft cloth. She felt that if she closed her eyes, she would sleep forever, floating along on a cloud.

Whenever the King was preparing to eat, Pia and Enzio were summoned to the dining hall, where food was laid out on a sideboard.

At first they were so daunted by being in the presence of the royal family that they could barely move.

"Go on, go on," ordered the King. "Taste!"

Pia chose a small morsel of melon, while Enzio selected a raspberry.

"No, no, more than that! Bigger bites!" ordered the King.

Pia munched her way through an entire slice of melon. Enzio ate a dozen raspberries.

The King and Queen and the royal children studied them as they ate. "You feel fine?" asked the King. "Go on, then, try that pork, that goose—everything—go on, big bites."

Enzio and Pia hesitated. Giovanna stepped into the room and walked the length of the sideboard, checking that the food was properly displayed. "Go on, you heard the King. Eat! Big bites!" Giovanna then whispered, "It's okay. I tried it all."

And so Enzio and Pia ate from each serving plate. They ate goose and pork and melons and raspberries and pecans and squash.

"Go on," urged the King. "Those sweet things, too."

Enzio and Pia ate chocolate-drizzled berries and sweet tarts and tiny cakes laden with cream.

"You feel fine?" asked the King.

Enzio, suppressing a burp, nodded.

Pia licked her lips. "*Very* fine, sire."

That evening, Giovanna brought new clothes for the tasters. For Pia she had a fine red smock, a crisp white apron, black hose and shoes, and a red ribbon for her hair. Enzio was given a new linen shirt, black hose and breeches, black shoes, and a black tunic with a red sash.

As soon as Giovanna left, the children donned their clothes.

"Ho!" said Enzio. "Wish we had a looking glass." He strode across the room, imitating the straight-backed Prince Gianni. "Do I look fine?"

"Truly fine," Pia said. "And me?" She minced across the room in tiny steps, imitating Princess Fabrizia. "Do I look fit to be among the royals?"

Enzio bowed, "Yes, Your High, Majestic, Royal Person."

Pia curtsied clumsily, unaccustomed to such sturdy shoes. "Thank you, Your Majestic Sire."

They gamboled around the room, bowing and curtsying and giggling until they were once again summoned.

"The King wants porridge before bed. Hurry, hurry."

This time they were summoned to the King's antechamber. He was seated on a leather-topped stool before a small, intricately carved golden table, above which hung the King's seal embroidered in silver and gold and red.

"What's this?" the King said. "They cleaned you up? You don't look so bad, cleaned up. Go on, then, taste!" He motioned to a side table on which sat a large serving bowl of porridge, a golden bowl for the King's portion and two smaller wooden bowls for the tasters.

When the King was satisfied that they had completed their duty, he said, "You feel fine? Off with you, then."

Pia hesitated. "King?"

"What? What?"

"Your seal there, the King's seal, what is that one thing there?" She pointed to the object in the corner, the one she and Enzio had not been able to decipher, the one that looked like a worm.

The King was affronted. "You peasants are not familiar with my seal?"

Enzio bowed, feeling that was a good apologetic gesture. "We are most familiar with your seal, but we do not know what that one thing is."

The King was impatient to eat his porridge. "That? That's a *corno*. You don't know what a corno is?"

Both Enzio and Pia put their hands against their chests, at the spots where their own coral cornos lay hidden.

"Oh!" Pia said. "A *corno*." She leaned closer, examining the seal. "I see that now."

◦ 34 ◦

Bother, Bother, Bother

The King, who had wanted an early morning nap so badly, was prevented from taking it when he was reminded that the Minister of the Daily Schedule was awaiting the King and Queen in the official chambers.

"Oh bother, bother, bother. Every day that man prattles on, telling us more things we have to do. I am the King! I am tired of people telling me what to do!" Grumbling in this manner, he nonetheless donned his itchy robes and allowed his Man-in-Waiting to place the heavy crown on his head, and he made his way down the stone steps.

No sooner had he and the Queen settled themselves on their thrones than the Minister of the Daily Schedule entered, trotting across the room in his pointed purple shoes, his round bulk swathed in orange and red silk and velvet. In one hand he held a sheaf of papers. With two fingers of his other hand, he stroked his curling mustache.

"Ahem, ahem," he began. "On today's schedule is—"

The King yawned. The Queen leaned back, ignoring the drone of the minister. She was thinking about her hermit, who had this morning been ensconced in her new quarters. The Queen had agonized over the Countess's warning that the hermit's lodgings should be spare. It would have been a much more enchanting place with new tapestries and fur throws and flowers from the garden. Lavender would have been nice, and some of those pale pink roses.

However, not wanting to appear ignorant of the ways of hermits, and bowing to the apparent knowledge of the Countess, the Queen had reluctantly ordered simple arrangements. The room was cleaned, a hay-filled mattress was draped with plain linen, and the floor was covered with rush mats. A dark oak table with a washing bowl, a sturdy chair, and wooden candleholders with tallow candles were the only other adornments.

The Queen had felt apologetic when she'd shown the hermit her lodgings, but she did not apologize, for a Queen does not apologize. She watched as the old woman stood in the center of the room, taking in the space. The calico cat made itself at home on the mattress, while the black cat stalked the perimeter of the room, sniffing.

"I hope you find this agreeable," the Queen said.

The hermit took one more look around the room. "A roof over my old head, walls, a corner to sleep."

The Queen did not know what to make of this response. Was the hermit satisfied, or was she disappointed?

From a bundle she carried, the hermit withdrew a wooden cross and placed it on the table, leaning its top edge against the wall.

"Would you like that hung on the wall?" the Queen asked. "I will send someone to hang it for you."

The hermit snorted in an undignified way. "*Puh*. I can hang it."

"Oh, well, then. I will let you settle in, and tomorrow we shall meet again here, and—and—begin?"

"Begin?"

"Yes," the Queen said, "we will—begin. I will come here and talk, and you will offer wisdom."

"Ah, wisdom."

The Queen made a hasty exit, not at all sure what to think of the old woman. This hermit business was more complicated than she had imagined.

In the official chambers, the Minister of the Daily Schedule was prattling on: ". . . and finally, the Ministers of Inventory seek an audience with Your Majesty." Relieved to be finished with his report, the minister looked up from his papers. The King was asleep, the

Queen inattentive.

"Ahem," said the minister, clearing his throat loudly, "ahem!"

The King grunted. The Queen blinked at the minister.

"Ahem, and finally, as I was saying, the Ministers of Inventory seek an audience with Your Majesty."

"What?" said the King. "What for?"

"I do not know precisely, sire."

"Have there been more thefts? Is that what they are coming to report?" This thought made the King extremely agitated. More thefts! He did not think he could bear it.

The Queen reached over to tap his arm. "Now, now, Guidie."

The minister was eager to flee the room. "I do not know, sire. Shall I add them to the daily schedule?"

The King pulled at the collar of his cape. "Oh, bother! Go ahead. Add them to the other things—the other things you said are on the schedule."

The King was depressed.

35

A Dream?

Having completed their breakfast-tasting duty, Pia and Enzio were exploring the interior courtyard, free until the King summoned them again. Enzio scooped a handful of polished white pebbles from the path. "Is this real, Pia? Are we really here and not in the dungeon?"

Pia regarded the enormous and glittering castle which hovered above and around them, like a vast stone god embedded with gems. Shafts of sunlight played on the stone, sending off brilliant glints and sparkles. Servants bustled to and fro, carrying sacks of laundry or wheat, while others groomed gleaming white horses.

Tall King's Men, in their red cloaks dappled with shiny gold medallions, stood at attention at every entry and high up on the stone walls, so high up they looked like red birds, their capes fluttering like wings in the wind.

"I don't know," Pia said. "It doesn't *feel* real."

Pia shuddered to recall their fear on the day she and Enzio had been snatched from the village and brought to the castle. That terrible ride seemed as much a dream as this idle walk through magnificent gardens. Her head was teeming with new images: of purple and red and gold tapestries, of gleaming marble floors, of tall golden candles, of the royal family in their silks and velvets and gold-embroidered gowns and tunics, of velvet slippers and crisp damask linens, and of the taste of rich foods—pheasant and cream and strawberries and chocolate. She patted her stomach, satisfyingly full for the first time in her life.

So sure this was a dream, so certain that it would evaporate as swiftly as it had appeared, Enzio had pocketed sweet rolls and slices of pork from the breakfast tray, which he now pulled from beneath his tunic, offering some to Pia.

She shook her head. "I am full of strange foods. I'm not hungry. Do you hear that, Enzio? I'm *not hungry*!" She laughed, so absurd did the words sound to her.

Enzio took a bite of the roll. "I feel like fat Franco!" He stuffed his mouth full of the roll and waddled about, imitating Franco.

Pia and Enzio were in the kitchen quarters nosing around, eager to see what delicious food was being prepared for the day. A servant girl, about Enzio's age, said, "You are the tasters?"

"Yes," Pia answered.

The girl giggled.

"It's funny?" Pia asked.

"We all taste," she whispered. "A pinch of this, a dab of that."

Enzio said, "And no one has ever been poisoned?"

The girl laughed, covering her mouth with her hand. "No. No poison. Not yet."

Pia liked the girl, with her free laughter and

her shining eyes. "Does the King know he has so many tasters?"

"Oh, no," the girl replied. "He thinks we merely cook. How can you cook without tasting?"

Pia thought of all the times she had taken meager bites of Master Pangini's food as she prepared it, feeling guilty for each stolen morsel.

Enzio reached for a slice of pear. "Why were we chosen? Why didn't the King choose some of you to be his tasters?"

The girl offered a bowl of newly shelled pecans to Pia. "No one knows. Some say it is because he does not trust us"—she frowned at the thought—"but normally he is a trusting soul. Too trusting. Some think it was Count Volumnia who put that notion in his head, not to trust us."

"Count Volumnia?"

The girl giggled again. "A plump chatterer who believes he knows everything."

"But why *us?*" Pia asked. "There are lots of people in the village. He could have chosen anyone."

"Like Franco," Enzio said.

"Franco?" the girl said.

"A plump chatterer, who thinks he knows everything," Pia said.

Later, when Giovanna was showing Pia and Enzio around the castle, initiating them in the whereabouts of all the entries and exits, hidden stairwells, and vast chambers, Pia asked, "Giovanna, what about our master—Pangini? He must have been as angry as an old goat when we didn't return. He must think we've run off."

Giovanna sat on a stone ledge, leaning against the wall. "You needn't worry about Pangini. I am sure he knows exactly where you are."

"How?"

Giovanna winked. "Pangini? You would be surprised what that Pangini knows." Giovanna was about to continue when a rustling on the steps below made her stop and listen. She put her finger to her lips, cautioning them to remain silent. "Come," she said, "let us continue exploring." She led them down a back stairway and across the courtyard and into an arbor laden with roses: pink and yellow and peach and white and red. Reaching a bench, Giovanna and Pia sat while Enzio trawled his fingers through the stones on the path.

"Giovanna?" Pia said. "Do you know of Signora Ferrelli?"

"Signora Ferrelli? Why do you ask?"

"We saw her here the first day. Is she a spy?"

"A spy? Mercy! A spy?"

"How do you know of her?" Pia asked.

"Child, just because we live in the castle does not mean we are ignorant of what goes on in the village. The King and Queen and royal children might be ignorant of such things, but we servants are not. Everyone knows of Signora Ferrelli, especially now, of course."

"Why?"

"She lives here now."

"What?"

"She is the Queen's hermit."

"Her *what*?"

"Her *hermit*."

“What,” asked Pia, “is a hermit?”

“Ah,” Giovanna said. “Let me tell you about the King’s hermit and the Queen’s hermit. . . .”

36

Peasant Ignorance

Castle children—those born to the cooks and groomsmen and ministers and any of the hundreds of other castle staff—were taught, from the time they could talk and walk, the appropriate ways to behave in the presence of the royal family. They knew their bows and curtsies; they knew to remain silent, to cast their eyes down; and they knew, especially, never to touch a royal personage. Only the Ladies- and Men-in-Waiting and the doctor and midwife, and a few of the stable boys who had to assist the royals in mounting their horses, ever touched the royals.

Pia and Enzio, naturally, had never been taught these things. They knew only of cautions regarding the King's Men, who, from time to time, were seen in the village. Pia and Enzio knew to be careful around them, and that girls should never speak with the King's Men unless directly questioned by one.

The first time Pia had seen Princess Fabrizia was when the Princess entered the dining hall and halted abruptly in front of Pia, regarding her with ill-disguised disgust. Pia was so stunned by the Princess's extravagant gown that she reached out to touch it.

The Princess recoiled. "What are you *doing*?" she demanded.

Pia reached out again to *touch* the dress. "I was only—"

"Stop! Do not *touch* me!" The Princess stomped her foot for emphasis.

"But I was only—what is that—what's it made of?"

The Princess opened her mouth wide, astonished at the effrontery of this peasant. "You are not supposed to speak to me, unless I ask you to." The Princess pursed her lips as if she'd been sucking on a lemon.

"Why not?"

The Princess stomped her foot again. "Stop that. Stop talking!"

Prince Gianni, heir to the throne, entered the room. "What is it?" he asked his sister.

"Her, that—that—peasant person. She's talking to me!"

Prince Gianni, who was more than familiar with the Princess's frequent tantrums over trivial matters, turned to Pia. Something about her struck him. He was rarely in the presence of peasants, rarely in the presence of the castle staff except for those who attended to him. Perhaps it was the strangeness of her looks, rather wild and unkempt. There was something in her eyes, dark pools which beckoned him. There was something in her stance, tall and confident, almost jaunty. She was not at all intimidated by the Prince, did not even seem to know that he was the heir to the throne.

"You spoke to the Princess?" he asked.

"Yes." Again she reached out to touch the Princess's gown. "I wanted to know what this is—it's so—so—"

The Princess could not back away fast

enough, pulling her gown from Pia's grasp. "See? See?" she said to her brother. "See how she does?"

Prince Gianni took his sister's arm gently. "The peasant is admiring your gown, and merely wants to know the name of the fabric. Perhaps she has not seen such a beautiful gown on such a beautiful princess before."

"But who is she and why is she here?"

"I am Pia, and that boy standing over there is Enzio, my brother."

"And why are you here?" asked the Prince.

"We are the tasters."

The Prince and Princess looked baffled.

Pia, thinking they had not heard her, said, loudly, "The tasters!"

"Oh," the Prince said, "I can't recall—"

He was interrupted by Prince Vito, who charged into the room, took one look at Pia and Enzio and said, "Don't talk to them. They're the tasters."

During Enzio's and Pia's first official tasting in the dining hall, the royal children stared at them. They had never before seen village peasants up so close, in their own castle.

Princess Fabrizia's nose wrinkled. The girl did not seem to mind that her hair was a riotous, untamed mass of curls. It made the Princess slightly ill to look at her. And the boy! She was deeply gratified that her brothers did not look like *that*. She admired the richly embroidered tunics of fine cloth that her brothers wore. She admired their clean, white hands. The Princess hoped that these taster peasants would soon be out of her sight.

Prince Vito squirmed in his seat. He wanted to dash upstairs, grab his sword, and challenge that boy Enzio to a duel. He would show that boy what a prince could do with a sword! He hardly noticed the girl, so intent was he on imagining Enzio cowering beneath his foot, a sword at his neck.

In contrast, Prince Vito's elder brother, Prince Gianni, barely noticed Enzio. Prince Gianni was too intrigued by Pia. He felt odd, as if a spell had been cast over him, rendering him mute. He watched the way she chewed a piece of melon, wiping her hands upon her smock.

He liked the way her hair, so thick and curly and jet-black, looked like skeins of soft yarn. He loved the way she smiled at her brother when she tasted the sweet cake. The Prince wished the smile were aimed at him.

After they finished their tasting and were dismissed from the dining hall, Pia and Enzio slipped back to their quarters, retrieved the sack and pouch which they had hidden there, and found their way outside the castle gates, roaming the exterior gardens, looking for a spot in which to hide the pouch. They wound through the gardens, too open and accessible for a hiding place, and followed a path that led to an unexpected tunnel of trees, which they entered.

"What do you suppose this is?" Pia said.

"A tunnel."

"I know, but what's it for?"

Enzio ran his hand along the tree trunks and gaped at the densely interlocked branches overhead. "What's any of this for—what's the castle for and the gardens and—and—all of it?"

Midway down the tunnel, they stopped.

"You thinking what I am thinking?" Pia asked, looking at the branches overhead.

"Most probably."

"Here then," Pia said, handing him the sack. "Up you go."

Enzio scrambled up a tree trunk and easily secreted the pouch amid the branches and leaves. Using a stone from the edge of the path, Pia carved a small squiggly mark on the tree's trunk, to mark the spot.

"Ho!" said Enzio. "You've drawn a *corno!* "

37

New Inventories

The Ministers of Inventory stood before the King, each of them grasping a rolled piece of parchment on which was recorded his or her latest inventory.

"Come, come," grumbled the King. "What is it now?"

As before, the ministers looked anxiously from one to another, hoping someone else would speak.

"Who is in charge here?" the King demanded. "Is there no Minister of Ministers of Inventory?"

The ministers looked blank.

Exasperated, the King bellowed, "You, there." He pointed to a sturdy, pink-faced man in the center of the line. "You are the Minister of Ministers of Inventory. I hereby appoint you. Now, speak!"

The man's pink cheeks deepened in color. He was flattered by the sudden elevation of his stature, but he was also flustered. "Sire, I thank you for the honor." He bowed and, in doing so, dropped his parchment. "Ahem. Ahem. Sire, we come to you with new findings."

"Which are—?"

"Ahem. I will begin, and, ahem, as before, we shall each report—"

The King did not think he could bear it. "On with it!"

"Ahem. Sire, I am the Minister of Inventory of Oats, and I report one extra sack."

The King wrinkled his brow. "What's that? An extra sack stolen?"

"No, sire, an extra sack in the inventory. One more than should be there."

"One *more?* And how might that be?"

"Sire, I cannot explain."

The King glared at the next minister. "You, then—and the rest of you—come on, then. Let's have it!"

A second minister reported that he detected two additional bolts of silk.

"What?" said the King. "Not two stolen ones? Two extra ones?"

"Yes, sire."

"And I," continued the next minister, "am the Minister of Inventory of Vegetables and I record four additional carrots, eight more radishes, and six extra potatoes."

"And I, sire, record a creamer lid, the very lid that had gone missing."

"And I, sire, detected six additional rabbits."

On they went, each having discovered surplus items: one rake, eight nails, seven knives, one pair of stockings, three chamber pots, and one cow.

"An extra *cow*?" blurted the King. "How can there be an extra *cow?* Where is all this coming from?"

In unison, the ministers shrugged, puzzled by the new findings, but also delighted with their discoveries. Surely the King would be happy?

The King, however, was dismayed. "Are you suggesting that the thief—or thieves—is returning things?"

Several of the ministers scratched their chins. The new Minister of Ministers of Inventory found his hands suddenly trembling. Was he supposed to have an answer? "Ahem. Sire, this is an important question. It is one we have not yet considered—"

The King slapped his hand against his knee. "Well, consider it!" he ordered. "Consider it!" He waved them away. "Off with you, off with you!"

When the ministers had departed, the King fled up the back staircase, down the hall, and into his bedchamber. He tossed his crown and cape on a chair and fell heavily upon the bed. *I will think about this later.*

ೞ 38 ೞ

A Duel

Prince Vito roamed the castle in search of the taster boy, whom he found outside the kitchen quarters. Enzio was licking chocolate from his fingers.

"You, taster boy!"

"What?"

"Bow!" ordered the Prince. "And do not speak until I ask you to."

Enzio thought this was a foolish game, but he didn't mind playing it. He bowed low, licked the chocolate from his lips and waited.

"Do you fence?" inquired the Prince.

"Fence?"

"Swords, fencing, like this—" Prince Vito

drew his sword and slashed at the air.

"What a fine sword." Enzio reached for it, barely touching the hilt before the Prince withdrew it.

"Don't touch! This is *my* sword, the sword of Prince Vito. You think you can handle one of these?"

"Couldn't be too hard," Enzio said. He had never held a real sword, but he had fashioned replicas from branches and had often dueled with Pia in the woods with their homemade weapons.

"Ha! I have trained for *years*. Did you hear me? *Years!* "

"And what did you learn?"

"Don't ask me questions. It's not permitted. Follow me."

In the dirt-floored Chamber of Swords, Prince Vito selected a weapon for Enzio. It was a simple and plain sword with no carving on it.

"Let's see what you can do with this," the Prince said.

The sword was heavier than the branch swords Enzio had held. He moved it through the air, assessing it. Prince Vito retrieved two chest guards and face masks from the wall and handed one of each to Enzio.

"What are these for?"

"No questions! You put them on, like this. Watch. For protection."

"Protection from what?"

"No questions! You shall see." The Prince stepped back and adopted a peculiar stance which made Enzio laugh. "What is so entertaining, peasant boy?"

"Name is Enzio. You look funny."

The Prince slashed the air with his sword. "*Funny?* You think I look *funny*? We'll see how funny you think I look when we're finished. *En garde!* "

"Eh? What?" Enzio watched the Prince step forward and back, left and right, a little dance. He mimicked the Prince.

Prince Vito smirked. "Clumsy!" he said, and with that, he thrust his sword at Enzio.

"Ho!" Enzio exclaimed, taking up the challenge. "Ho!" He parried the blow, ducked and slashed back, the metal of their swords clanging sharply in the air.

Prince Vito quickened his steps, slicing at Enzio's sword, but Enzio leaped to the side. Around the room they went, engaged in their duel, from one wall to the other, leaping over trunks, sliding in the dirt, whirling and stabbing, clanging swords, evading and parrying.

"Take that!"

"And that!"

"You're done for!"

"Not yet!"

They had worked up a sweat when they were interrupted by Giovanna.

"Enzio, the King wants his tasters!"

Reluctantly, Enzio laid down his sword. "Want to do that again?"

The Prince did not notice that Enzio had asked him a question. "Tomorrow! We duel again!"

After Enzio left, Prince Vito continued around the room, slashing at an invisible opponent. He had been astonished by Enzio's prowess. The peasant was not elegant in his technique, but he was agile and daring, and far more skilled than the Prince had expected.

39

The Heir and a Hair

Prince Gianni stood on a balcony gazing down at the courtyard, where servants wandered to and fro. A small gray-and-yellow bird flew lazy circles in the air, amid the perfume of lavender and hyacinth. The Prince had been standing there for some time, not sure why, until he spotted Pia crossing the courtyard. He realized then that he had been waiting for her. *A Prince does not wait for anyone or anything.*

He watched as Pia climbed a low stone wall and walked its length. Was she singing? She sat on the wall and held out her hand. The bird circled her and landed on her palm, pecking at it gently. The Prince had never seen such a thing before, a bird landing on someone's hand.

Pia looked up, scanning the castle walls, and when she spotted Prince Gianni, she called out. "Hey! Prince!"

Servants stopped to stare at her, shocked at her boldness. They followed her gaze upward to Prince Gianni, who was so stunned at this effrontery that he froze, mouth agape.

"Prince!" Pia called again. "Hello!"

Prince Gianni, aware of the stares of the servants, awkwardly raised his hand briefly in acknowledgment and then stepped back into the shadows. He should have been insulted by the girl's impropriety, but instead he was captivated and slightly dizzy.

He started down the steps, reconsidered, climbed them again, and paced the hall. Once again he descended the steps and, adopting a casual but princely stance, he entered the courtyard, striding purposefully toward the stables. He was disappointed that Pia had vanished. As the Prince continued across the courtyard, servants bowed. He did not speak to them; it was not expected that he should. He entered the darkened stables, unable at first to see, his eyes adjusting to the dim interior. He had no immediate interest in the stables; it had been simply a reason to cross the courtyard in hopes of seeing Pia.

"Hey! Prince!"

She stood midway down the corridor, in front of the stall which held his horse. The Prince thought he should correct her, instruct her to curtsy and to address him in the proper fashion, but something prevented him from doing so.

"That's my horse," he said.

"He's a beauty," Pia said. "Look at how white he is and how shiny his coat, and look at these eyes. I could fall into them."

The Prince studied his horse, seeing him in a new light. He was handsome, it was true.

"What's his name?" Pia asked.

"Zelo."

"Zelo. Hello, Zelo." She stroked Zelo's forehead and leaned her head against the horse's neck.

No one was supposed to touch the Prince's horse except Zelo's groomsman or the Prince, but the Prince remained silent, watching Pia, moved by her open affection for the animal.

"You're fortunate," Pia said. "You can do whatever you like."

"Pardon?"

"You have this beautiful horse, and you can ride Zelo whenever you want."

"But I have duties, obligations—"

"Oh, *puh*."

"'Puh?'" he echoed.

"You could ride right now, if you wanted to."

"But you," said the Prince, "you are the one who can do what you want and say what you want."

A servant called from the stable entry. "Taster! The King wants his tasters!"

To the Prince, Pia said, "It seems I have an *obligation* right now," and off she went, dashing across the courtyard.

The Prince stroked Zelo's forehead as Pia had done. On Zelo's neck was a long, dark, curly hair. The Prince removed it, examining it. *Pia's hair.* As he curled it around his finger, Zelo's nose nudged his hand, as if he, too, wanted the single hair of Pia.

40

The Queen and a Bean

Outside her hermit's door, the Queen paused to gather her thoughts. She had lain awake much of the previous night trying to imagine what she might say on this first meeting. There was so much to express, and yet she could not divulge it all at once, could she? Perhaps she should not say anything. Perhaps she should merely listen and absorb the wisdom of the hermit. She wished she knew how the King handled his hermit. She wanted to ask him, but he might scoff at her weakness. He might say, "You are the Queen. You handle your hermit however you like."

Now, outside the hermit's dwelling, the Queen wondered if she should knock at the door, or if she should, as Queen, boldly enter. Normally, someone opened doors for her. While she was contemplating this, the door opened. The Queen stepped inside. The calico cat came directly to her, nuzzling the hem of her gown. Across the room stood the black cat, watchful. The door closed behind her, revealing the slim, bent figure of her hermit.

"Hermit! I am here." The Queen was bewildered by her own awkwardness. Her eyes surveyed the room, settling on the single chair. She sat, arranged her gown, and looked up at the hermit, only then realizing that there was only one chair in the room. Where would the hermit sit? "I see we need another chair. I will request one."

The hermit said nothing.

I can hardly give her the only chair, thought the Queen. *I am the Queen, after all.*

"What is it you want, then?" asked the hermit.

Her raspy voice and her bluntness disoriented the Queen: "Want? Why, I want nothing." This was not true, the Queen realized. She wanted so much from the hermit, but she could not put into words what she wanted, and it would be unqueenly to admit to wanting anything.

"Then why are you here?" asked the hermit, who remained standing. "Why am I here?"

The Queen was annoyed. *A hermit ought to know what a hermit does*, she thought. Gathering her wits and relying on instinct, the Queen said, "I understand you are wise, and that is why you are here, and I am here to partake of your wisdom."

"Wisdom?" the hermit said. "Ah, wisdom. Some might say that no man—or woman—is wise at all times."

"But I gather you are wise *most* of the time."

"The wind in one's face makes one wise."

"I see." The Queen did *not* see, not exactly, but this sounded wise, and she was delighted that the hermit was offering wisdom so soon.

"Do you? You understand that?" the hermit asked.

Embarrassed, the Queen could not admit that she did *not* understand, and so her mind raced to make sense of the old woman's words. "The wind in your face—why, that's like difficulty, yes? And if you face difficulty, you—you—oh, I have it! If you face difficulty, you learn. You become wise? Is that it?"

The hermit winked.

The Queen had expected more, perhaps praise or approval. She did not like this feeling of ignorance. "I suppose you think I do not often have the wind in my face," she said to the hermit. "It might seem that way to you, or to outsiders, but I have known my share of wind."

At this, the hermit nodded, and the Queen took it as her cue to continue. "Shall I tell you about the wind I faced when I was young? I was not always Queen, you know." The hermit's passive silence urged the Queen onward, allowing her to speak of things she had never before voiced aloud. Once she began, memories and thoughts and feelings poured forth like a stream overrunning its banks.

The hermit settled herself on the mattress, leaning back against the wall. She punctuated the Queen's talk with occasional nods, as if she understood and accepted what the Queen was saying, but the hermit uttered no words of her own until the Queen, who was speaking of her youth and of her life before privilege, began to sob.

The hermit rose and came to the Queen's side. "There, there," the hermit said, patting the Queen's arm. That simple touch undid the Queen, who buried her face against the old woman's waist, clutching at her coarse garment. When the Queen finally collected herself, the hermit said, "You see? The wind in your face has made you wiser than you know."

The Queen did not feel wise. "I'm not sure why—not sure what—has come over me. I should leave you now. I have duties to—"

"Ach, duties!" said the hermit. "Be careful you do not waste your life on duties."

The Queen looked up at the old woman, overwhelmingly grateful for her presence and for this final pronouncement, which struck with such force that the Queen felt it lodge in her chest.

The hermit reached into her pocket and withdrew a bean, which she handed the Queen. “See this? A small bean. A quiet, unassuming bean, and inside is so much. Here, you have it.” The hermit pressed the bean into the Queen’s hands.

A *bean*? The Queen stared at it, so smooth and simple. She closed her fingers around the bean. “I have much to think about,” she said as she took her leave.

Outside the hermit’s dwelling, the Queen heard the door close behind her. Ahead of her lay the hornbeam tunnel and beyond it the high, glittering walls of the castle. The Queen wanted to remain in the tunnel. She did not want to leave its cool and serene enclosure. She wanted to think about the bean.

41

The Peasant and a Pheasant

At first, Pia and Enzio returned to their room or to the interior courtyard between tastings, not knowing when the next call might come. Quickly, though, they became used to the King's hunger schedule, and discovered that if they remained within shouting distance, the time in between their tasting duties was free. Free!

Never before having had the luxury of so many idle hours, Pia and Enzio were eager to explore. They roamed the hidden stairways, skipped through the stables, amused the goats and chickens, trolled through acres of cloth in the sewing rooms, sniffed flowers, climbed trees, watched the blacksmiths heat iron and shape horseshoes. Up and down and in and out they roamed.

One afternoon, while Enzio was riding in the hay cart, Pia exited the main castle gate and walked around the castle's perimeter. To one side of the main gate were the King's Men's stables, the outer gardens, and, below, the hermitage. To the other side was the tunnel of trees. Pia was familiar with this side of the castle. Skirting the castle walls, Pia strolled around the back, where she discovered vast garden plots stretching to the outer walls. A dozen servants dotted the rows, weeding. At the far end stood a row of tall Lombardy poplars surrounded by bushes.

A pheasant stepped out from the bushes, peered left and right, skittered along the edge of one bush, stopped, listened, and shook its tail feathers. The bird then abruptly retreated into the undergrowth.

Pia followed the well-trodden path between the garden plots, making her way toward the bushes. Around her the air was filled with the pleasant hum of the servants' murmurs and the occasional calls of birds dipping in and out of the trees. Pia slipped into the bushes, parting branches and stepping over low vines.

She might have stepped on the pheasant, so well-camouflaged was it among the leaves and low branches, but the pheasant made its presence known with a flutter of wings and a strange, high-pitched *weenk* call. *Weenk. Weenk.*

"I won't hurt you," Pia said soothingly. "Is this where you live?" Rustling from behind the pheasant alerted Pia to the bird's mate, only her eyes and beak visible amid the branches. "Are you nesting?" Pia asked. "Are there eggs or babies already?" The first pheasant, which Pia took to be the male, stood still, watching Pia as she knelt and put out her hand. "I have no crumbs with me, I'm sorry to say."

The pheasant bobbed his head, as if in understanding, and once again shook himself, releasing one of his long tail feathers. The bird stroked the feather with his beak and then picked it up and extended it toward Pia.

Pia took the long feather, brown with

chestnut and gold markings. "Thank you, I am most honored," she said. Behind the male, the female's head was cocked, studying Pia.

Pia wondered about this pair, nesting so close to the castle. Was it comfortable for them? Was it safe? Could they leave? "Be careful," she called as she retreated. "You don't want to end up as dinner."

She walked back up along the garden plots, pausing here and there to wave at the servants or exchange a few words. She felt uncomfortable, strolling along while they were working. She was inclined to offer her help, but then the booming voice of a cook's helper called out: "Taster! Taster, the King summons you!"

Clutching her feather gift, Pia raced back to the castle. She was relieved to have a job to do.

A Story Was Told . . .

42

A New Story

It was a quiet, warm evening, and as the royal family waited for the tasters to complete their sampling of the evening meal, the King was looking forward to a few empty hours, with no visitors to entertain and no meetings to attend.

The Queen was subdued, unusually so.

"Are you well, my queen?" the King asked.

The Queen was watching the tasters munch roasted chicken and lick their fingers. She felt as if a sparrow were fluttering in her chest.

"Gabriella?"

The Queen pressed her hand to the bodice of her dress. "Mm? What was that, Guidie?"

"Are you well? You seem . . . not yourself."

The Queen gazed around the table, taking in Prince Vito, Prince Gianni, and Princess Fabrizia. Her children were preoccupied with watching the tasters, too. "I do feel a little strange," she replied.

The King reached for her hand and tapped it lightly. "Perhaps you should retire early?"

He thought he was being quite considerate, and so he was startled by his wife's answer.

"Oh, no, Guidie." the Queen said. She withdrew her hand and twisted her napkin, agitated. "Let's have some diversion this evening. How about—oh, I know—let's have the Wordsmith tell us a tale."

"The Wordsmith?" The King saw visions of his idle hours fly out the window. "This evening?"

"Oh, Guidie, please?"

"Of course, dear. If you want the Wordsmith, the Wordsmith you shall have." He shifted to his children. "Gianni? Vito? Fabrizia? We shall have a tale tonight."

"What did you say, Father?" Fabrizia asked.

Prince Gianni and Prince Vito reluctantly turned to their father.

"What?"

"What?"

The King was not used to such inattention. "What has come over all of you?" He glanced at the tasters. Could his family be more interested in the peasants than in him? "We are having the Wordsmith tonight, that's what I was saying. The Wordsmith. A tale. Your mother wishes it."

"Maybe the tasters can come, too," the Queen said.

"The tasters?"

Pia swallowed a bite of creamy tart and said, "Oh, Your Majesty Sire King, we would like that very much."

Prince Gianni appreciated Pia's nerve, but Prince Vito scolded, "Do not address the King."

"Now, now, Vito, they do not know," said the Queen.

"Someone should tell them, then," Prince Vito said.

"Tell us what?" Enzio asked.

Fabrizia pointed at the peasants. "See? See how they do?" This time, though, she was not bothered. Their behavior amused her. She had warmed to them, in part because they were an audience for her, observers of her lavish gowns and dainty ribbons, and in part because they were different from anyone she had met before. She was both puzzled and intrigued by the girl's behavior, so bold and unladylike. As for the boy, now that he was cleaned up, he looked handsome, in a crude, peasant way, she thought.

The King turned to Pia and Enzio. "Have you tasted everything?"

"Yes, Your Fine Majesty."

"And it was good?"

"Most good, Your Fine Majesty."

"Well, then, off with you."

Prince Gianni said, "Father? The tasters? Will they join us this evening for the tale?"

"Gabriella? Are you sure you would like them to be present for the tale?"

"Yes, Guidie."

"Tasters, we will summon you when it is time for the Wordsmith."

Pia and Enzio did not know what a wordsmith was, but they had a vague sense of what a tale was.

"Will it be like Franco, do you think?" Enzio asked his sister. "Gossiping about the villagers?"

"Might be. Or maybe gossip about the servants in the castle? Or the royal family?"

"I don't think anyone could do *that*, not in their presence."

"I wonder why he is called a wordsmith."

"Maybe it's like a blacksmith, who makes things from iron. Maybe a wordsmith makes things from words."

The royal family was in the antechamber, seated in a semicircle on chairs laden with colorful cushions. Behind them were two empty chairs, to which Pia and Enzio were ushered by a servant. As soon as they had seated themselves, a man entered.

Enzio elbowed Pia. "*Ooh!*" he said. "The Wordsmith?"

Pia was spellbound by the man's swirling black coat and his mysterious demeanor.

"Sire?" asked the Wordsmith. "What do you desire in your tale this evening?"

"*Mmph.* A noble king."

"Queen Gabriella?"

"I'd like to think a minute," she said.

"Prince Gianni?"

"A poet," he said, "and—and—a girl."

"Prince Vito?"

"A duel! Swords! Horses!"

"Princess Fabrizia?"

"A young man—not a prince—and—and—a lovely princess'—she put her handkerchief to her cheek to cover her blushing—'a princess who *does something*."

"And our guests?"

"What?" Pia said.

"Is there anything you would like tonight's tale to include?"

"Like what they said?" Pia asked. "You mean, like kings and poets and swords? We can choose things to be in the tale?"

"Aren't you going to tell us about things that already happened?" asked Enzio.

"Don't they know what a tale is?" Fabrizia asked.

"If you tell me what you'd like to hear about," the Wordsmith said, "I will include that in my story. It will be a new story, created especially for this audience tonight."

"How are you going to do that?" Pia asked. "How are you going to know what to say?"

The Queen said, "Perhaps you'd like merely to listen this evening, to see how the Wordsmith creates his miracles?"

"No, wait," Pia said. "Can you put anything at all in the story?"

"I can," replied the Wordsmith.

"Even, say, a—a—cabbage?"

"Yes."

"I'd like a cabbage in the story."

"A cabbage?" Fabrizia said. "A *cabbage?*"

Enzio waved his hand at the Wordsmith. "Oh, and I'd like a—a—snake!"

The King squirmed. He was regretting

having asked the tasters to join them for the evening's tale.

"Agreed," the Wordsmith said. "A cabbage and a snake."

"And, and—wait!" Pia said. "Two orphans, a brother and a sister. Can you put them in the story?"

"And a pouch!" Enzio blurted. Pia gave him a warning look, but Enzio barreled on. "A pouch, and the orphans find it."

Princess Fabrizia frowned at the tasters. "That's probably enough," she said.

"Very well, then," said the Wordsmith. "I believe we have sufficient ingredients, unless the Queen would like to add anything."

"I would like to add a peasant woman."

The King took her hand, but the Queen's eyes were on the Wordsmith, who was opening his velvet bag. The King made note of the fact that the bag he had seen at the hermit's had been returned to the Wordsmith. The King wondered how that had been accomplished. Had the hermit summoned a servant? Who had the hermit spoken with?

The Wordsmith now closed his bag and looked up at the audience and began:

Not so long ago and not so far away there lived a noble king. . . .

꩜ 43 ꩜

The Castle's Tale

At night, as the air cooled, strange sounds came from the castle walls: creaking and groaning, alternating with low moaning and soft sighing, as if the walls were telling their own story as they settled down for the night.

These sounds had frightened Pia and Enzio on their first few evenings in the castle.

"Sounds like ghosts wailing," Enzio had said.

"Or someone crying."

"Or there—hear that? Someone sighing."

When they had asked Giovanna about the sounds in the night, she'd replied, "I know. No ghosts, I don't think. It's more the castle itself. It's alive."

"Not really alive?" Enzio said. "Not like people?"

"I'm not so sure," Giovanna said. "It feels alive to me. It makes noises during the day, too, but usually we can't hear them because there is so much other noise."

"Then it's very sad," Pia said. "They're not happy sounds."

"Ah, but listen in the daytime when the sun is shining on the walls. Put your ear up to the stone. You may hear a different sound then."

The next day, Pia and Enzio had done just that, put their ears to a castle wall. The wall was warm and rough, and at first they heard nothing and felt foolish. Then, as they leaned there, what they heard amazed them. A soft humming, a pleasant, soothing sound, emerged.

"Ho!" Enzio said. "You hear that? Like a song, almost."

Pia patted the castle wall. "If it does have a tale to tell, I wish we could hear it."

On the night they heard the Wordsmith's tale, they lay awake, listening to the lament of the castle walls. Pia knew she would not sleep. Her mind was racing with the words of the Wordsmith.

"What a strange thing he can do," she said. "How does he *do* it?"

"Might be that bag of his. Magic inside, maybe."

"But all those words—and he only looked in the bag once, before he began, and while he was talking, I forgot where I was. I thought I was floating somewhere else. I thought I was the orphan in his story."

Enzio agreed. "Me, too. But sometimes, when he was talking about the king, I felt like I was the king, and then when he was telling about the peasant woman, I felt like her, too. It made me dizzy."

"Enzio? When he talked about the pouch—"

"About the orphans finding it! I was afraid. I thought he was inside my head and he knew what we'd found."

"But then he said they buried it under a stone."

"We didn't do that."

"And the pouch in the story had different things in it."

"The keys. That was magnificent when they found out those were keys to the castle and they were really royal children!"

"I wished it was us," Pia said.

"Me, too. And the peasant woman, the one who becomes the queen? And she turns out to be their mother? I was wishing—"

"I know, I know," Pia said softly. "I was wishing it, too."

"And the poet—don't you think he was a lot like Prince Gianni?"

Pia considered this. "Yes and no." The way the Wordsmith had described the poet, he *looked* like the Prince, but the poet in the story said beautiful things. He told the orphan girl her hair was as soft as a downy bird. She had liked that part.

"And, oh," Enzio said, "it was so funny about the prince throwing the cabbage at the snake. I thought I would laugh myself right out of my seat!"

Pia giggled, remembering. "But it wasn't real."

"The story? He said it wasn't, but how could he tell it, if it wasn't real? How did he know what to say?"

"Enzio? It's like when we pretend we're a prince and princess, and we live in a castle. We make it up, out of the air."

"Do you think we could tell a story like the Wordsmith's?"

"What—with a king and queen and cabbage and snake and orphans?"

"No, with other things."

"Whatever we want? I'll start," Pia said.

Not so long ago, and not so far away, there lived—a—a—fat master.

Enzio beamed in the dark. "My turn now," he said.

And the fat master was extremely ugly, and he was forever shouting things—

Pia interrupted:

Like "you dirty cabbages!" and "you filthy beetles!"

Once they got going, they rushed on, snorting with laughter as they passed the story back and forth, long into the night, drowning out the moans and sighs of the castle walls.

ഽ 44 ഽ

Restless

Princess Fabrizia was restless. She had already summoned her Lady-in-Waiting to bring an extra blanket, and then again to remove it, and then to squash a spider. She couldn't get the Wordsmith's tale and the tasters out of her mind. The tasters had reacted to the story at every turn: they guffawed; they gasped; they clapped. It had seemed rather uncivilized at first, but then her mother and her eldest brother were laughing, too—not so much at the story, but at the tasters' infectious laughter. Princess Fabrizia had found herself paying more attention to the story, to see what it was that made Enzio and Pia react as they did.

It wasn't until she was lying in her bed that she realized the story was not entirely flattering to the princess in it. The princess in the story had seemed spoiled and sometimes mindless, always flitting about in a new gown. Princess Fabrizia reddened at the recollection. *Was that me? Am I like that?* Always, before, she had loved to hear tales of beautiful princesses in beautiful gowns. Why was this story different? She wondered if it was because of the orphans in it. The Wordsmith had made them brave and maybe even more important than the princess in the tale.

She wasn't sure what to make of the end of the story, either, with those orphans finding out they were really royal children. Enzio and Pia, however, had loved that part, clapping loudly and shouting out "*Ooh!*" and "Bravo!" Princess Fabrizia wondered how she would feel if she suddenly found out that a couple of orphans were her siblings.

Prince Gianni's thoughts, as he lay in bed, were similar. He imagined that Pia and Enzio were the orphan children and that, like the children in the story, they were really royal—not from his own family, but from another royal family—and if so, that would make Pia someone who—he blushed to think of it—would certainly be eligible to be his wife.

Prince Vito was already asleep, dreaming of duels. Enzio was with him, and the two of them were comrades, fighting off the enemy, who were throwing cabbages at them.

King Guido, too, was already sound asleep, but not dreaming. The story was not on his mind because he had not heard much of it. He had dozed off.

The Queen was not asleep, nor was she even in bed. She was standing at a narrow window which looked out onto the courtyard, and she was weeping. The Wordsmith had looked into her heart and offered her salvation. The poor peasant woman in the story was herself, she was sure, and when she married the future king and saved the villagers from starvation, the peasant woman was a heroine.

The Wordsmith was strolling in the garden,

emptying his head, bound for the King's hermit's cottage. He knew they would have another visitor joining them tonight: the Queen's hermit.

The castle did not sleep, either. It sighed and moaned, and even, once, seemed to laugh softly in the dark night.

And all the while, the leather pouch rested comfortably in the cool leaves of the hornbeam tunnel, a black hair lay tucked in a silk handkerchief beneath Prince Gianni's pillow, a chestnut-and-gold feather reclined in Pia's shoe, a small bean nestled in the palm of the Queen's hand, and a black snake slithered quietly through the garden.

45

The Mission

In the kitchen storeroom, Enzio watched the Minister of Inventory of Vegetables. The minister held a scroll and a piece of charcoal, with which he marked his tally of vegetables.

"Seven, eight. *Mm*. Eight turnips." He made a mark on his scroll and frowned. "Oh, dear. Six missing."

Enzio peered over the minister's shoulder. He couldn't read the scribblings, but they intrigued him. "Minister? We had turnips last night, with the pork. Probably six."

"Well, then!" The minister was cheered. "That accounts for it!" The minister counted twelve cabbages. "Oh, dear. Four extra ones."

"Minister?" Enzio said. "Some were freshly picked this morning."

"Oh? That's it, then." The minister altered his tally. "It is not so easy, all this inventorying, you know. Things coming in, things going out. One minute there are two cabbages; next minute there are twelve; turn your back again and someone's taken away three cabbages for cooking!"

"It must be hard to keep track," Enzio said.

"You can't imagine! It's not so easy, not so easy. And think of the other ministers—trying to keep a tally of nails or spoons or cows."

"Cows? That shouldn't be so hard. Cows are, erm, so *big*."

"They hide, behind the bushes."

"So," Enzio said, "you mean it might appear that something is missing when really it is misplaced or has been eaten or—or—is hiding in the bushes?"

"Precisely!"

"Does it matter, if your inventory is exact?"

"It didn't used to matter, but recently the

King has become rather agitated about our inventories." The Minister of Inventory of Vegetables shrugged. "I try my best."

Pia rushed into the storeroom. "Enzio, Enzio, we are summoned!"

"To taste?"

"No, it's the Queen. Quick!"

The Queen had awakened with a mission on her mind, and servants were dashing to and fro in the wake of her orders.

"Oats, vegetables, milk, chickens!" she called out. "Flour, eggs, pork! Gianni, see that Fabrizia and Vito are ready. Pia? Enzio? You're coming, too. Quickly, now!"

"Coming where?" Enzio asked.

The Queen was already hustling to her chamber. "To the village!"

She had, technically, informed the King of her mission, but he was, as she'd anticipated, still in his morning fog.

"What's that, Gabriella? Going to the village?"

"Yes, dear. I'd like an outing. And—and—I may take a few things along—trifling things—for the villagers."

"But Gabriella, I was going to see my hermit this morning."

"Now, now, Guidie, of course you have to see your hermit. *Most* important." She leaned close to him. "Guidie, I will have the children and the King's Men with me. You do not have to come."

The King brightened. "Oh! *Hrmph.* Well, my dear, if you insist—"

"Of course," she said.

Once the King was safely off to his hermit, the Queen had set the castle bustling with her orders. "Piles of food!" she said. "Quickly, quickly!" And as the King sat comfortably in his hermit's dwelling, out of the castle gates poured the Queen, the royal children, the tasters, twenty King's Men, thirty servants, and sixteen wagons filled with food.

The mood of the troupe was festive. No one but the Queen knew what had prompted this mission, and no one, including the Queen, knew how they would be received, but it was a dazzling morning, with the sun glittering off the castle at their backs and flickering off the wide Winono River which lay before them. The carts rumbled, the servants hummed, the horses neighed and pranced.

Prince Gianni rode beside his mother; Prince Vito and Princess Fabrizia followed, all on their gleaming white horses. Behind them rode Pia and Enzio on two chestnut steeds, the children struggling to stay upright. Surrounding the royals and the tasters were the King's Men in their red cloaks emblazoned with gold medallions, and in a long, trailing line behind came the servants and the carts laden with food.

46

A Favor

"Hermit? I need to do something kingly."

The King's hermit sat across from him, hands folded gently in his lap. "Kingly?"

"Yes, something *noble*—or daring and bold. In all the Wordsmith's stories, the king does something noble."

"For instance?"

"The king has the *answers* to the problems. He makes things better. Like this thief business—in a Wordsmith story, the thief would be found."

"And what would the king do with the thief?"

The King was going to answer, "Kill him!" but when he thought back on the Wordsmith's stories, the king usually forgave the thief, or if the thief died, it was because someone—often a prince, rarely the king—had overzealously stabbed him, realizing too late that the thief was—it was strange to recall this now—the thief was often guilty of such a small crime, like stealing a loaf of bread to feed his family.

The hermit repeated his question. "And what would the king do—in a story—if he found the thief?"

"You would think the king would kill the thief and that would be that, but in those stories the Wordsmith tells, I admit, I feel a little sorry for the thieves."

"And why is that?" asked the hermit.

The King detected a tawny fur ball on the hermit's smock. He wanted to reach out and touch it. It looked like fox fur or cat hair. "The thieves, they don't take much. A loaf of bread, a sack of oats. Their families are hungry. Of course, it is wrong to steal, especially from the

King! People can't go about stealing whatever they want."

"I suppose you're right," said the hermit. "After all, the King is always right, is he not?"

"Of course," said the King, although as soon as he said it, he knew it was not true. How could a King always be right? How was he to know what to do?

The hermit said, "Sire? I wonder if I might ask a favor of you."

The King was rattled. A favor? He was waiting for wisdom and did not like being interrupted for a favor. "What, then?" he said. "What sort of favor?" The King could not disguise his impatience.

"I would like to meet the tasters, if Your Majesty does not object."

"The tasters? You want to meet them?" It was an odd favor. No harm in it, the King supposed, but still, odd. He did not think to ask *why* the hermit wanted to meet the tasters, so preoccupied was he with his own concerns. "Fine, fine, if you wish."

"Thank you."

The King sat still, waiting, hoping that wise words would now come from his hermit. The hermit closed his eyes—a good sign that wisdom would soon flow—and breathed in and out deeply, slowly. When at last he opened his eyes, the hermit said, "If one's head is in the clouds, one cannot see the gold at his feet."

Gold? thought the King. He instinctively looked at his feet, but all he saw there were a few tawny hairs, which he reached for absently. "Ah, yes," he said, accepting this apparent nugget of wisdom, but inwardly he was disappointed. *Clouds? Gold? What has that got to do with noble deeds?* As he took his leave of the hermit, he wondered if the Queen's hermit was easier to understand.

47

An Unexpected Reception

Down the hillside streamed the castle troupe. On horseback, the King's Men, bedecked in their red cloaks, encircled the Queen, the royal children, and Enzio and Pia. Behind them rumbled the carts loaded with food and accompanied by servants walking alongside. Overhead, the sky was as blue as the cornflowers which dotted the hillside, only a few pure white puffs of cloud adorning its dome. Red poppies and yellow buttercups grew wild among the blue cornflowers and tall grass, all of them waving in the gentle breeze.

"A perfect day!" exclaimed the Queen.

Pia lifted her face to the sun, cherishing the air, so clean and warm on her cheeks. She was so high up on her horse, so far from the ground, so much closer to the sky.

Prince Gianni glanced at Pia, who was gazing upward. He followed her gaze, noting the blue of the sky and the whiteness of the clouds. He didn't often look up at the sky. Now he wondered why that was. It looked spectacular.

Princess Fabrizia was watching Enzio. He looked so fine on his horse, so strong and handsome. She was confused by her interest in the taster boy, and she was also resentful that Enzio was not looking at *her*. Instead, Enzio's attention was on the servants who walked near his side. In fact, he was smiling at one in particular: a young servant girl. *A servant girl!*

Prince Vito wanted to break free and ride ahead, to escape the group and race wildly along the banks of the river and on to the woods. He wanted Enzio to join him. The two of them would ferret out hidden danger and save the kingdom.

Down, down the hill they all came, a wave

of people and carts surrounded by the glittering King's Men. Before them lay the sparkling, winding Winono River and the bridge which led to the village beyond.

Clip, clomp, clip, clomp, over the bridge they surged. Pia noted the water, so clear, reflecting the sky so perfectly that the clouds seemed to be floating in the river.

It was not until they neared the far side of the bridge that she wondered what the villagers would make of this scene, and what they would think, seeing her and Enzio riding among the castle throng. She tried to imagine what she might have thought if she were still living in the village and if she had never lived at the castle.

I would be awed, she thought. A visit from the royal family! But it also occurred to her that she might be embarrassed, for she would not have had time to clean herself up, nor find her best smock. Always before, the villagers had received ample warning when the royals were coming. They had always had time to prepare themselves, to clean the streets, to gather flowers to offer to the Queen and the Princess.

Enzio, too, was wondering what the villagers might think. He thought they would be proud to see him—a mere peasant—among the royals, and on horseback, no less. He was eager to see the surprised looks of the villagers.

When the first wave of King's Men and the Queen and Prince Gianni cleared the far side of the bridge, a group of peasants near the river shrank back, startled by the flood of people approaching. Some slid into doorways to hide themselves, and one young boy cried.

The Queen raised her hand in greeting, a delicate royal wave, but the peasants did not smile and curtsy as they always had before. They seemed stunned, disoriented.

"What is the *matter* with them?" she asked Prince Gianni. "And why are they so dirty?"

The Prince could not answer her. He, too, was mystified by this reception.

On into the narrow streets poured the castle group, a vast swell surging through the streets, as peasants withdrew from its glittering, clattering mass.

"What is the matter with them?" repeated the Queen.

Although she did not answer the Queen, Pia understood what was wrong.

"Stop!" ordered the Queen. "Stop!" She was speaking to the King's Men in front of her, who instantly halted, shouting orders for all to halt. To the nearest servants, the Queen said, "Give them some food."

Unsure as to how to accomplish this, the servants were tentative, offering a few melons or apples to bystanders, who still hung back, reluctant to take the offerings.

"Prince Gianni," pleaded the Queen. "Tell them what to do."

"Uh. *Erm*."

Prince Vito, frustrated by his brother's inaction, swerved out of the line and rode up and down, alongside the trailing carts. "Go on," he said, "tell them it's free." He turned to the frightened peasants. "Free! Take it!" He reached for a sack of wheat and threw it to a young boy. "Take it!" The sack landed at the boy's feet. "Take it!" ordered Prince Vito. The boy, obeying, snatched the sack and raced down an alley.

The servants, intimidated by Prince Vito's boisterous orders, began tossing sacks out of carts, aiming them at the feet of the villagers. Soon it was a chaotic scene, as other villagers, beckoned by the noise, arrived to see what was happening and quickly realized that if they did not grab the food, they might miss out.

It had been the Queen's plan to ride on through the village, through its winding streets, passing out food in an orderly way as they went, but they were stalled, crowded on all sides by villagers clamoring for food. Some broke through the ranks of King's Men and leaped into the wagons, throwing the contents to friends and neighbors. Flying through the air were fruits and vegetables, chickens, and sacks of oats and wheat. The peasants, who had been so timid and stunned at first, were now noisily shouting to each other, the din frightening the horses and making them skittish.

"Oh!" said the Queen. "I don't understand—"

"I want to go home," whimpered the Princess.

Out of the crowd, a man shouted, "Hey! It's the antelope boy and the eagle girl. Pangini's wards! Up there, see?"

A boy hooted. "Hoo! What are you doing up there?"

Pia and Enzio, who had both smiled at the first recognition, were shaken when a woman hissed at them. "Ssst. Spies!" she said. Others, suspicion and distrust in their eyes, ogled the pair.

"It's us," Enzio tried to explain. "We're the tasters—" But his words were drowned out by catcalls and by villagers bellowing for food. It had become a frenzy of snatching and grabbing. Some villagers raced off with their booty as others returned with wheel-barrows to load up the goods.

In a tiny voice, the Queen said, "It's not—it's not—what I expected."

48

Interrupted

The noise in the village streets was deafening: people shouting, horses neighing, sacks of food thudding to the ground, crows shrieking, dogs barking. The King's Men had formed a tight circle around the royal family, but Pia and Enzio found themselves outside this circle, their horses rearing and thrashing.

As her horse spun, Pia glimpsed two familiar figures lumbering down the street: Master Pangini and Franco. Franco was shouting to Pangini, and as her horse came around again, she saw Franco point at Enzio and then at her. She was not sure what expression she expected to see on their master's face, but it was certainly not the one she glimpsed. It was not anger or distrust or disgust. It was more like jealousy and resignation.

Pia was confused, but she did not have time to ponder further, for someone was roughly yanking her from her horse. "Hey!" she shouted. "Hey!"

It was Prince Gianni, and he had pulled her onto his own horse. Swiftly he steered free of the crowd and off he rode, his horse clattering close along the sides of buildings.

"But—Enzio—" she said.

"He is safe," the Prince said. "Vito has him."

Ahead Pia could see a tight circle of King's Men racing the Queen and the Princess across the bridge. "But—Enzio?"

"There," said Prince Gianni, shouting above the noise. Pia could feel the warm breath of his words against her neck as she followed his gesture. Vito and Enzio were racing close behind them, and they were laughing, as if it were all a game.

"And the servants?" Pia asked.

"They'll be fine. They'll be along as soon as the carts are empty."

As they dashed over the bridge, Pia trembled. She was reminded of the last time she had been carried off on horseback over this bridge, when she and Enzio thought they were going to the dungeon. But in her tremble, too, aside from fear, was the warmth of the Prince's breath on her neck and the feel of his arms around her waist. It was not an unpleasant sort of trembling, and yet she stubbornly wished she had rescued herself. She had not needed a prince to rescue her.

Across the bridge, the King's Men stopped, awaiting Prince Gianni and Prince Vito. As the two princes joined the group, a lone King's Man thundered down the hill, coming from the castle.

"The King! The King!" shouted the man, alarm in his voice. "The King! The King!"

"What?" the Queen begged.

The King's Man pulled up sharply beside the Queen. "Come quickly, Your Majesty. The King is ill."

"Ill? How so?"

"Poisoned!"

49

Hermit in the Tunnel

Not long after the Queen and her entourage had departed for the village, Signora Ferrelli and her cats emerged from their darkened hermitage. They were about to enter the hornbeam tunnel when a servant stopped them.

"You're not to go there."

"Oh?" Signora Ferrelli said. "And why not?"

"It's the Queen's place. It's her own tunnel."

"Ah. Her own tunnel, you say?"

"Only the Queen goes there."

The Signora peered into the arched bower of trees which formed the tunnel. "And who keeps it so finely clipped, and the path so neatly swept?"

"The gardeners, of course."

"So, they, too, enter the tunnel?"

The servant look perplexed. "Only to trim it, that's all."

After the servant departed and was out of sight, Signora Ferrelli entered the tunnel with her two cats, the calico one trailing her ankles and the midnight-black cat striding ahead, acting as the hermit's sentry.

The Queen's hermit inhaled the scent of the leaves overhead and admired the long rows of slim trunks, the overarching branches, and the long, cool expanse of the tunnel. She walked the entire length of the tunnel slowly, and then retraced her steps. Her black cat darted ahead of her and leaped up a slim trunk, climbing into the branches above.

"What are you after, cat?" the Signora said. "Have you found a tiny bird?" She stopped to watch the cat clamber through the branches, idly wondering about the Queen's visits to this tunnel. The hermit could understand its appeal. It was so quiet and cool and silent, so comforting.

A twig fell onto her head. "Cat?" She could hear the animal pulling at branches and leaves. "Are you tangled? Cat?" She briefly glimpsed his green eyes and the dark fur of his face and a tawny object dangling from his mouth. "So, you have caught something?"

The cat scrambled back down the tree and dropped his catch at the hermit's feet.

"Well, well, well. Look what cat has found." As she reached for the leather pouch which lay at her feet, the cat placed one paw on the pouch, possessively. She bent to stroke the cat. "Good cat, good cat. Let me see what you have found."

50

Poison

The Queen was understandably distraught as she raced back to the castle. *The King! Poisoned!* She was terrified that she would lose her dear Guidie, and she was also racked with guilt. *If only I hadn't left. If only* the tasters had been there. She felt a sharp pang, for if the tasters had been there, then it would be they who were poisoned. She was shocked by how deeply she cared and mortified that she had not considered the possibility of their endangerment before now. *But Guidie, dear Guidie. Who would do such a thing to my Guidie?*

Pia and Enzio, too, were overtaken with

guilt. They should not have left the King. It would have been better if they had been poisoned, but neither Pia nor Enzio wanted to be poisoned, and so they were grateful that they were not now dying. Pia wondered about Giovanna. *She would have tasted the King's food, wouldn't she? Was she poisoned, too?*

Through the castle gates the group raced, sending up clouds of dust. Servants huddled in the courtyard. Some of the women wept. The Queen and her children, and the King's Men, and Enzio and Pia rushed into the castle, up the stone staircase, and into the King's chamber. The King was retching violently into a pail. The smell of the King's vomit assaulted them. Surrounding the King were his doctor, his Man-in-Waiting, and four nurses.

"Oh, Guidie!" At least he was still alive.

"His condition is most grave," said the doctor soberly. "Most grave."

"But when? How?"

"After his meal. Poison, no doubt."

The Queen turned to her eldest son. "Gianni, please—"

Prince Gianni, with uncharacteristic determination, took charge. "I will investigate," he said. "Vito, come with me. Pia, Enzio, you, too. Fabrizia, you stay here."

Princess Fabrizia, torn between wanting to escape the dreadful smells and wishing to be near her parents, wept into her handkerchief. "No," she said abruptly. "I want to *do* something. I'm coming with you."

Prince Gianni swept down the staircase, across the courtyard, and into the kitchen, with the Princess, Prince Vito, and Pia and Enzio in his wake. At the far end of the room, four King's Men surrounded Giovanna, who was seated at the table, weeping.

"Oh, Pia, Enzio," she said. "It is terrible, terrible."

Prince Gianni moved quickly. "Who served the King his meal?"

Giovanna sniffed. "I did."

"And did you not taste it first?"

Giovanna stood, her face flushed. "But I did, I did. I tasted everything."

Prince Vito interrupted. "How can that be?

How is it that the King is poisoned and you are not?"

The King's Men regarded Giovanna suspiciously.

Pia stepped through the throng and placed her hand on Giovanna's arm. "Tell me what he ate."

"His meal. He ate all of it."

"But tell me what foods," Pia urged. "Exactly."

Giovanna sniffed, trying to control herself. "Three melons."

Princess Fabrizia stepped forward. "Three slices of melon?"

"No, three whole melons. I tasted each one first. They were especially sweet, and the King was quite taken with them."

"What else?" the Princess asked.

"Strawberries and blackberries. The whole bowl."

"The big serving bowl?" Pia asked.

"Yes. I couldn't taste every berry, of course, but those I did taste were so delicious."

"And what else?" the Princess pressed.

"A chicken. The whole chicken. It was so tender, the King said. And six or seven turnips, I believe. Eight or nine potatoes. Wine—I tasted that, too. And for dessert, the raspberry tart—"

"The whole thing?" Pia asked.

"Yes, it was so divine, the King said. Oh, and another tart, the apple one, with chocolate sauce, and—" Giovanna stopped. "Oh, do you think—?"

Princess Fabrizia and Pia exchanged a glance. They had already arrived at their conclusion. The Princess took Pia's hand in her own.

"Mercy!" Pia said. "I think the King might be suffering from an overdose of food."

51

Beans

When the Queen was assured that the King was indeed not poisoned but was, instead, suffering from overindulgence, she made her way to her hermit's cottage. She could barely contain herself, so overflowing with thoughts was she, and so in need of wisdom. As soon as the Queen entered the dwelling and saw the still, silent figure of Signora Ferrelli, her words poured out. She described the trip to the village and the distressing reception and consequences.

"I was only trying to help," she said.

"You thought they would be grateful?" asked the hermit.

"Of course, and happy—"

"But they were not?"

"No. They were—it is hard to describe—like animals! They were dirty and rude and . . ."

The hermit was sitting on the edge of her mattress, her calico cat cradled in her arms. "Did they know you were coming?"

"No, it was a surprise."

"Ah," said the hermit, "a surprise." She stroked the cat gently. "And do you remember when you were a girl? Remember what you told me the other day?"

The Queen blushed at the recollection of her outpouring. "Yes, but I don't see—"

"Do you remember saying that you, a poor peasant, were coming back from working in the fields when a young man—a prince—rode up to you? You were carrying—what was it in your apron?"

"Beans," the Queen said.

"Ah, beans. And you were dirty, were you not, from working in the fields? And embarrassed that the young man should find you so?"

The Queen was beginning to understand where the hermit was heading. "I wished I had had time to prepare."

"And you were rude to that prince, were you not?"

"I was."

"And remember when you said that he dismounted from his horse and offered you a token, a necklace—do you remember how you felt?"

"I snatched it from him," the Queen said. "I was angry at him."

"And why were you angry?"

The Queen leaned back in her chair, trying to remember that day. "Because I didn't like that he had such things and gave them away so freely, whereas I and my family—we had only dirt and beans." She stared at the hermit. "Ah! I see. I see."

"Do you?"

"I think so. The villagers were confused, maybe they were embarrassed, and oh!—" She reddened to think how foolish she must have looked, high on her white horse, bestowing food: the rich woman showering trifles on the poor peasants. The Queen groaned. "I have made a terrible, terrible mistake."

"Maybe not," said the hermit. "Did you not ultimately fall in love with that prince? And marry him? And become his queen?"

"Of course, but—"

"And were you greedy at first for all the things the prince had? For the food, the clothes, the castle, the gardens?"

The Queen was ashamed to recall her younger self. "I was."

"And did you feel you deserved to have those things?"

"Yes!" the Queen answered. "Why should only the royals have them? Why couldn't my family have them? Why shouldn't everyone—?" The Queen stopped, aghast. "Oh dear, dear, dear. What must the peasants think? How could I not understand that?"

The calico cat slipped from the hermit's arms and sauntered over to the Queen, who reached down and picked it up, letting it rest in her lap. The cat was warm and comforting, soothing to the troubled Queen.

"I think you have had much wind in your face today," the hermit said. "And I think you are much wiser as a result. You agree?"

As the cat purred in her lap, the Queen said, "Yes. I think you are right."

52

The Summons

When a servant relayed the message to Pia and Enzio that they were summoned to the King's hermit's dwelling, they were, of course, surprised.

"Why?" Pia asked.

"I am not told."

"Giovanna said that only the King may go to the hermitage."

The servant clasped her hands together. "True, but you are summoned. The King knows."

Pia and Enzio walked slowly through the castle gardens, following the curving path. They stopped at the granite bench.

"Enzio? I am thinking that the hermit is supposed to be wise, yes?"

Enzio was raking his hand through the gravel at his feet. "Yes."

"And so it's likely he can read, yes?"

"Probably."

"Enzio? Let's ask him about the parchment in the pouch. Let's ask him what it says."

"He is the King's hermit, and he will wonder how we got that paper, won't he? What if it is an important document that belongs to the King?"

"Then we will tell him the truth. We will tell him we found it."

"Maybe we should ask the Wordsmith instead."

"The Wordsmith? But who can we trust more, the hermit or the Wordsmith?"

Enzio considered the question. "I am not sure." As he sifted through the gravel, a black snake emerged from beneath the bench and slid slowly around Enzio's feet.

"Ho!" Enzio said. He and Pia were startled, but not afraid. They had encountered plenty of snakes in the woods and had even met a few in Master Pangini's hut. The snakes did not bother anyone, and besides, they ate mice, which were more of a nuisance in the village than snakes were.

The snake crossed in front of Enzio and Pia before slowly making its way across the path and into the bushes on the far side.

"The snake is a sign, don't you think?" Pia asked.

"Of what?"

"Of something hidden—that emerges."

"We'll get the pouch."

They made their way to the tunnel and entered it, running their fingers along the trunks until they spotted the one that Pia had marked with the squiggle of a *corno*. Enzio scrambled up into the branches.

"Pia," he called. "Do you see anything from down there?"

Pia examined the leaves overhead. "No, you hid it well."

"I thought so," Enzio said, "but it's not here."

"Enzio, don't fool." She watched as he raked the branches and leaves with his fingers, shaking the canopy. All that dropped were a few stray leaves and twigs.

Enzio searched thoroughly. "Pia, it's gone."

As they arrived at the hermitage, Pia and Enzio felt they had let someone down, but who that someone was, they did not know. Downcast, they knocked at the door, which immediately swung open.

Not only was the King's hermit standing before them, but also two guests: Signora Ferrelli and the Wordsmith.

"Enter, enter," said the King's hermit, ushering them inside. "You know the Queen's hermit, Signora Ferrelli?"

"We do," Pia said.

"And you have met the Wordsmith?"

"We have," Pia said. "It is only you we have not met."

The hermit smiled. "Ah, but you *have* met me, child. You have."

53

A Noble Prince, A Peasant Girl

On the night after Enzio and Pia visited the King's hermit, they joined the royal family for a tale from the Wordsmith. They had been specially invited, as had the King's hermit and the Queen's hermit. When the King entered the room, the guests were already assembled, but he took scant notice of who was there because he was still feeling weak from his recent bout with overindulgence. He had only been able to sip clear broth ever since.

The Queen, however, knew who would be in the audience, for she had consulted with the Wordsmith about the tale he would tell. Prince

Gianni sensed an unusual tingle in the air. Prince Vito's mind was on duels. He and Enzio had dueled that afternoon, and the Prince was hoping for another skirmish the next day. Princess Fabrizia could barely sit still in her seat, so tempted was she to gape at Enzio.

Pia felt as if her blood were full of tiny bubbles. She was eager to hear the Wordsmith's tale. Part of it she had heard the day before, in the hermitage, but she knew there was more to the tale which the Wordsmith would relate.

The Wordsmith cleared his throat, peered into his black bag, and began:

Not long ago, and not far away, there lived a noble prince.

The King stopped the Wordsmith. "You haven't asked us what we want in the tale."

The Wordsmith glanced at the Queen before replying. "Pardon, Your Majesty," he said to the King, "but I thought I would not trouble you this evening for suggestions. I believe you will enjoy the ingredients I have chosen."

"But you began with a prince. Usually you say, 'There lived a noble king.' Have you forgotten the king?"

"Pardon, sire, you are correct. I have begun with a prince, but the prince may become—in this tale—a king. A noble king."

"Ah, very well, then, continue."

The Wordsmith told of a noble prince who meets a young peasant girl coming home from the fields, carrying beans in her apron. The prince is enchanted with the girl and offers her a necklace, which the girl takes, but rudely.

This fact was particularly heeded by Princess Fabrizia, who interrupted the Wordsmith's tale to say, "She doesn't behave very well."

"She is embarrassed," the Queen said. "That's why she is behaving that way." Princess Fabrizia gaped at her mother, puzzled by her defense of the rude peasant.

As the Wordsmith continued the tale, the King, instead of dozing off as he usually did, sat upright, listening intently. When the Wordsmith described the noble prince, the King interjected, "Why, that's like me, when I was young." He was charmed by this element in the story. "And that peasant girl, why, that's like you, Gabriella."

The Wordsmith related how the young prince and the peasant girl fell in love, and how she left her family and her kingdom to come to the prince's castle. "It was not easy for her, leaving her family behind, never to see them again."

"Oh!" Princess Fabrizia said. "Why not?"

"Her parents died shortly thereafter, of influenza. Her sisters and brothers, one by one, succumbed to various illnesses. They were poor people, with inadequate food."

"Oh dear," the Princess said. "It's so sad."

The Queen dabbed at her eyes with her handkerchief.

The tale continued. The listeners learned that the young prince's parents also succumbed to illness and that he became the young king and his wife the young queen. The Wordsmith spoke of a happy time for the pair, and of the births of their three children, and as he described each of the young children, Prince Gianni, Prince Vito, and Princess Fabrizia recognized the similarities between the children in his tale and themselves.

Enzio whispered, "Is it them he's talking about? The King and Queen and Gianni and Vito and Fabrizia? It's them, isn't it?"

"Maybe," Pia said, "but it is a story, remember."

Next, the Wordsmith told of the king acquiring a hermit shortly after Vito was born. "This was a kind king," the Wordsmith said, "and only the noblest of kings knows that wisdom must accompany leadership."

The King was flattered by this revelation. "Excellent, excellent," the King said. "Carry on, Wordsmith. An excellent tale you tell this evening."

Prince Vito was the only restless member of the audience. A prince, a princess, love, children, a hermit. Where were the duels? The enemies?

54

The Hermit and the Orphans

In the antechamber, a fire crackled in the fireplace and the candles flickered. The Wordsmith reached for his goblet and sipped slowly, refreshing his throat and preparing himself for the rest of his tale. When he continued, he told of the king's meeting with the hermit. Pia and Enzio listened intently, for this was the part of the tale they had heard the previous day. They wanted to see if they had heard it correctly.

"And so," the Wordsmith continued, "the king agreed to assist the hermit in settling his family obligations."

Afraid that the Wordsmith might omit

details, Pia said, "Wordsmith, what sort of family obligations?"

"Ah, yes. The hermit had two grandchildren. Their father had collapsed and died in the fields, and their mother had died during the birth of the second child. The grandfather, fearing that he had little to offer the children, arranged with the king that he would be the king's hermit if the king would agree to find a home for them, and that when they came of age, the children would be brought to the castle to be apprenticed."

The Queen and Prince Gianni looked at Pia and Enzio who, in turn, were gazing at the hermit. When Pia took her eyes from the hermit, she saw the recognition dawning in the Queen's and Prince Gianni's minds.

"Wordsmith," Pia said. "How did the grandfather hermit know the king would keep his word?"

The King blurted, "The King always keeps his word!"

"Yes," said the Wordsmith. "This king offered the hermit a written promise, as discussed, along with two of the king's golden medallions and four coral *cornos:* two that the children would wear and two that would be held by the hermit as proof, in addition to the document and the medallions, of this promise."

Enzio leaned forward. "But did the children in your story receive the *cornos?*"

"Ah, good question, Enzio. The hermit, fearing someone might convince the children to relinquish their *cornos*—so young were they at the time—deposited two of the *cornos* with a trusted elderly woman who lived in the village."

Signora Ferrelli winked at them.

"And there came a time, when the children were older, that the elderly woman gave the *cornos* to the children—"

"But wait," Pia said. "Wasn't there a pouch, too? You didn't tell about the pouch."

"What's she talking about?" asked the Princess. "How would she know what was in the story?"

Prince Vito slumped in his chair. "Aren't there going to be any duels?"

"Ah, the pouch," the Wordsmith said. "Duels! Thank you for reminding me."

And so the Wordsmith livened his tale with a description of a frightening thief in the night and a stolen pouch, and a duel fought between one of the young princes and the thief. "In a noble gesture," the Wordsmith added, "the prince spared the life of the thief."

"'Noble gesture'? That's good, that's good," Prince Vito said.

"But was there really a thief?" asked Pia.

"There was a man, yes, who looked like me, dressed in black—like me—who set off on horseback with the pouch, but perhaps he did not steal the pouch. Perhaps he was given the pouch by the king's hermit and perhaps he was taking it to the grandchildren. And perhaps someone with a vivid imagination called out, "Thief!" and so everyone *assumed* there was a thief."

"What?" Prince Vito said. "What do you mean, 'perhaps'—is the thief a thief or not?"

"I am confused by all these perhapses," said the King.

"And wait," Enzio said. "Do you mean that the man—who looked like you—maybe was not a thief and was trying to give the pouch to the grandchildren, the ones who actually found it? So maybe they didn't find it accidentally; maybe it was meant for them to find?"

"Isn't there going to be a princess in this story?" Princess Fabrizia said. "It's getting too muddled. I think you need a princess who does *something*."

"*Hmm*," the Wordsmith said. "I see the problem." And so he continued his tale, allowing the thief to be a real thief and the prince to fight a duel and catch the thief, and the Wordsmith also included a lovely young princess who not only convinced the prince to spare the thief's life, but who also saved the life of the orphan boy.

"And the eldest prince?" Prince Gianni asked. "You didn't say much about him."

"The gentle one?" said the Wordsmith. "He was a poet, kind and noble like his father, and he saved the orphan girl."

"In a duel?" asked Prince Vito.

"Of course, of course, a tremendous duel, with both princes fighting a crowd."

Pia preferred the original version of the story. "Wait, then," she asked. "Are you *sure* the prince saved the orphan girl? Maybe *she* saved *him*. Did you ever think of that?"

"What's going on?" the King asked. "I am getting a headache."

"Now, now, Guidie," soothed the Queen. "It will soon be over. Wordsmith, are you going to say how the king and the queen and their children and the orphans and the hermits ended up?"

"Yes." And so the Wordsmith told how the royal family opened the castle gates to the villagers and shared the bounty of their fields and how no peasant ever went hungry again, and how they all lived happily ever after.

Or at least mostly happily, most of the time . . . when there weren't duels and thieves and such. The End.

55

A Tale Ends

The Wordsmith completed his tale to a round of hearty applause.

"'Mostly happily, most of the time,'" said the Queen. "So nice, that ending, don't you think, Guidie?"

"I liked the beginning the best. There was more about the young prince who becomes a king in that part."

"I loved the part about the princess!" gushed Princess Fabrizia.

"The duels, those were good," added Prince Vito, "but next time there should be more."

Prince Gianni joined in. "I think there should have been more about the poet prince.

He sounded like a deeply interesting character."

"The orphans—that part was especially good," Enzio said.

Pia, standing beside the King's hermit, said, "And the grandfather hermit—I thought that was a nice surprise."

"But in the story tonight, it wasn't really a surprise, *bellissima*," the hermit said.

Signora Ferrelli tapped the Wordsmith's arm. "You forgot to mention that the elderly woman was not always so elderly, and you forgot to say that she became the queen's hermit. You forgot that part."

"Oops, so I did. Please accept my most sincere apologies."

Princess Fabrizia stamped her foot. "Wait, wait. How do they know the story?"

The Wordsmith looked sheepish. "I had some help with this one," he admitted.

The King said, "It was a fine tale, Wordsmith, and maybe one day you will get it completely perfect."

One might think, since the Wordsmith had completed his story, that the story ended there, but that night, surrounded by the castle walls which sighed and moaned and gurgled, each of the listeners of the Wordsmith's tale encountered remnants of the tale—words and images and characters—floating through their minds.

The King and Queen lay awake wondering if the castle gates *could* be opened to the villagers. Prince Vito wondered if there could be a tale solely of duels, with no soppy feelings in it, but he also wondered about that *noble gesture* the Wordsmith mentioned. He would have to think about that, about why it was noble not to kill the thief. Princess Fabrizia cried to think of children without a mother or a father.

Prince Gianni's mind raced as he attempted to reconstruct the Wordsmith's story. He wanted to be able to tell a tale like that, to string words together in such a way. Could he learn to do it? And could he learn to be a noble king? And could a king also be a teller of tales?

56

Ever After

Pia and Enzio listened to the sounds of the castle walls.

"Moaning," Pia said. "Hear that? It seems sad."

"Pia? The orphans in the story, they still do not have a mother or a father."

"But they have a grandfather, Enzio."

"Like us."

The castle walls emitted a soft sound, a light expulsion of air.

"Enzio? What did you think of what Grandpapa said about Master Pangini?"

"Which part? About being disappointed in how Pangini treated us? I felt sorry for

Grandpapa. He looked sad to hear it."

Pia reached for her pheasant feather and stroked it. "He was happy, though, that Signora Ferrelli scolded Master Pangini from time to time! And what about when the Signora said that she'd heard that Pangini *misses* us—"

"Ho! *Misses* us? He misses someone to cook for him and clean up after him, Pia. He's a mean, old, snarly—"

"Dirty, paltry beetle!"

Pia retrieved the lock of hair with its purple ribbon from beneath her pillow. "Funny about this lock of hair, Enzio, that the King put it in the pouch. What was it the Wordsmith said? 'A lock of hair from his firstborn child—'"

"'The grandest assurance of his promise.' Pia? Should we give it back now, the lock of hair?"

Pia slid the hair back under her pillow. "No one said anything about giving it back." Pia sat up. "Enzio, we can show our *cornos* now!" She pulled hers out of her gown and studied it.

Enzio did the same. "They will protect us."

"Maybe so, Enzio, maybe so."

"Pia, will we always be tasters?"

Pia considered this. "Oh, no, I don't think so."

"But what, then? Do we have to go back to the master and clean his hovel? Become servants in the castle? Or, wait, marry a prince and become a queen? Marry a princess and become—what?"

"Ugh! We will never go back to the master—Grandpapa promised—and I would not want to be a queen if I had to be polite all the time or trudge around in all those heavy clothes."

"But if you were a queen, you could say what you liked, and you could do what you liked, and the food is so tasty, Pia."

"So what will become of us, Enzio?"

"Maybe we could be hermits—"

"Who don't have to stay indoors—"

"—hermits who ride white horses—"

"—and feed the goats and chickens—"

"—and eat fine food—"

"—and give some to the villagers—"

"—especially the children—"

"—but not to Pangini—"

"—or Franco. . . ."

Pia felt as if she could soar out through the window and across the river and swoop over the village and dip and dive. The walls of the castle murmured low, mysterious tones, teeming with intrigue and possibility. Pia listened for some time and then began a story:

Not long ago and not far away, a young peasant girl and her brother kneeled in the smooth, gray stones on the edge of the river . . .

Also by Sharon Creech, and winner of the Carnegie Medal

13-year-old orphans Dallas and Florida had given up believing in such a thing as a loving home. But when an unusual couple ask them to live in the beautiful Ruby Holler, wonderful and magical things start happening.

'A delightful fable'
Sunday Times